ONE NIGHT WITH A GRUMP

AN AGE GAP SINGLE DAD BILLIONAIRE ROMANCE

JEWEL STEIN

1

SCARLET

I took a deep breath before I pressed the phone tighter to my left ear and spoke in a shaky tone, "Yes, Nana, I'm just on my way back; I promise I'll deal with the bills tomorrow."

The sky was roaring in the rather far-off suburban area just outside Crescent City in Northern California. It had cramped streets, and I had a feeling I would get sick if I stayed outside for a second longer. As it started to pour outside, my eyes drifted toward a rather tiny-looking bar with warm lights glowing inside and a jukebox sitting in the corner; tables were lined up at the back, and a man in a hat was sitting by the piano.

As soon as I stepped inside, a little bell rang above my head. I looked around, and the bar was pretty cozy. I slowly shrugged my heavy winter coat off my body and placed it on the rack to the side. I had barely even made my way toward the wooden bar across the small area when suddenly I heard heavy footsteps to my right. My eyes instantly landed on three men, drenched in rainwater from head to toe, drunk as they stumbled inside the bar. The first one instantly winked at me as he smirked, shrugging off his coat. I gulped as the anxiety rose to my chest.

Before I could get up and make my way to the door, the men had already approached me. One of them placed his left hand on the top of the bar. He smirked as he made a point to stare at me from top to bottom. I stayed quiet and tried to remain calm until I heard him speak; his words were slipping from his mouth, and I could tell he was extremely drunk.

"What do you say you come sit with me and my friends at our table? Drinks on us?"

He was still smirking, and his gaze made me want to throw up.

I shook my head, trying to be as calm as possible. "Actually I was just leaving...,"

He laughed. "Honey, you're not going anywhere; it's pouring out there..."

He reached forward to grab my arm, and I instantly took a step back, stumbling over the bar stool right behind me. Before I knew it, I was falling. I was trying to make sense of what just happened when I heard another voice: a more deeper and heavier one.

"The lady said she doesn't want anything to do with you. Did you not hear her?"

My eyes landed on perfectly styled jet-black hair, broad shoulders, and a Rolex shining on his wrist. I couldn't see his face. His elbow rested upon the surface of the bar as a drink sat in front of him untouched. I felt a sudden sharp pain rushing through my body. Before I even had the chance to try and pull myself back to my feet, I noticed from the corner of my eye that the same man with the ugly crooked smile had started to take a step closer to me. At the moment, I felt as if anxiety had attacked my whole body, and I could not move.

In an instant, the rather handsome man by the counter lifted himself from the bar stool. He seemed to know what he was doing. The man hovering over me stepped back as soon as his eyes landed on the handsome stranger. The stranger was easily a good five inches taller than me. He hovered over the three drunken men. One of them tried to take a step closer to him, and that was when the stranger lifted his hand. Before any of them knew what was about to hit them, it was already too late. His fist collided with one of the shorter men's jaw. I winced at the scream which erupted from his mouth. His body fell toward the bar stool on the right. The stranger stood still with confidence pouring from him.

The two other men rushed toward their friend, and the stranger turned toward me. I was surprised when he knelt carefully, offering me his hand. At that moment, my eyes met with his, and I realized he had emerald green colored eyes. The man was easily twice my age and sophisticated. My hand slipped into his, and before I knew it, he had easily lifted me, almost as if I didn't weigh anything.

My hand still gripped his as he turned to face the three men. He cleared his throat. "If I see you around here ever again, consider yourselves dead."

His tone was heavy and laced with dominance.

I had no idea what was going on; he refused to let go of my hand. I watched as the three men ran from the bar one after the other.

My breath slowed when he turned and came face to face with me. Our eyes met, he refused to look away and I was not one to be shy of eye contact. He cleared his throat and gestured toward our hands; they were still intertwined, and suddenly, a light shade of rose pink flushed through my cheeks. I loosened my grip on his hand.

"Are you okay?" he asked.

I nodded. "Yeah, I mean it's all thanks to you. I mean God knows what would have happened if you weren't there...."

I trailed off before I could say more when my eyes landed on the glass resting on the bar. Whiskey on the rocks, he had barely even taken a sip. I felt guilt rushing through my body. He noticed the change in my expression and spoke,

"Are you sure you're okay? You certainly seem shaken up."

I pointed to his whisky and laughed. "I just realized you didn't even take a sip of your drink at all because of all this."

I knew my voice was shaky. I was still in shock from what had just happened, but I was trying my best to remain calm. My eyes gazed over him. He didn't even look toward the glass; instead, his eyes remained fixed on me.

A few seconds passed in silence. "I'm a slow drinker; I like to take my time."

I saw a smirk dancing upon his lips. I was trying my best not to let my gaze linger at his lips for too long. There was something about the olive-green-eyed stranger that made me want to stay in his presence.

I had just registered what he had said when my ears were filled with his deep voice again. "If you don't mind me asking, what is your name?"

I responded quickly, "I'm Scarlet. And you are?"

The stranger was no longer going to be just that. I was hoping to get a name to attach to the face I couldn't seem to keep my eyes off of. It took him a moment, almost as if he was letting my name sit on his tongue for a minute.

"Scarlet, I must say it's an ordinary name. I'd like to think mine is a little out of the blue." He paused. "Damien."

He had a rather flirty smile on his lips. Before I could say anything else or divert the attention from the fact that my cheeks had started to blush, he gestured to the bar and said, "Would you like to join me for a drink? It seems today has been a lot for you."

The tone he had picked up made my heart skip a beat. He seemed empathetic and caring but cold and distant at the same time. I knew that after what he had just done for me, refusing just a drink with him would seem rude, and besides, the storm hadn't fully slowed down outside. So I offered him a firm nod, and we both made our way toward the bar.

As we reached the bar, the gentleman made sure he pulled out a stool for me.

I sat down, he gestured toward the bartender. "Can the lady please have a whiskey on the rocks as well?" He hadn't finished. He turned to face me and continued, "Unless you would like something lighter?"

This time a smirk appeared on my lips. I was not one to let go of a challenge, and I definitely was not a lightweight.

I shook my head with confidence and said, "I'll take the whiskey please."

I could tell his expression changed. He seemed surprised but had too much ego to show it openly.

The glass was placed before me, and both of us picked our glasses up at the same time. Eye contact remained as he lifted his glass higher, and I did the same.

"I guess it's a "thank you" toast for saving me back there," I said.

Before the glass could even reach my lips, the sound of my cell phone ringing flooded the small bar. I offered the man an apologetic look before I picked up my phone. I didn't even need to see the caller ID to know who it was.

"Nana, I think the storm is dying down finally. Don't worry; I'm coming back, and I will deal with the bills situation."

I knew I had to go. I slowly got up, and placed my phone back in the pocket of my winter coat. I turned to him, but that was when I noticed he handed the bartender what looked to be a hundred dollar bill. I raised an eyebrow; his glass was still on the bar untouched, but he stood up next to me.

"You know, I was going to pay for you, as a thank you. I'm sorry I can't really stay; longer my Nana is a little protective of me with the storm and everything..." I trailed off when I noticed a smile dancing on his lips.

He gestured toward the door. "Let me drop you off to your house safely. I feel as if your grandmother is right to be Leary of the people around here."

I didn't know how to react. A part of me knew that the storm hadn't fully died down yet, and walking would take longer to reach my place anyway.

I sighed and decided to trust my gut. "You can drive me back."

He escorted me toward the parking lot outside the bar. As he walked beside me, I couldn't help but notice that he seemed to be twice as cautious of his surroundings. His posture had changed, his shoulders were high, and his back was straight. He kept looking around, almost as if doing double takes. I wondered if he was looking for the drunk men from the bar or if it was something else.

A new Audi in jet black was parked by the corner of the bar. He held the door open for me before he got in on the other side.

Damien seemed like the type who didn't talk too much. His eyes were fixed on the road, and he checked the rear view mirror every few seconds. I gave him the directions to my apartment building, and as we stopped outside, something inside me changed.

He helped me from the car, I was moments away from walking into my place when I stopped and turned to him.

The words left my mouth without giving me a chance to think about them. "Would you like to come inside? The least I can do is offer you some tea."

The same flirty smirk was back on his lips. He raised his eyebrows before I heard the click of the car doors locking. He gestured toward the entrance of the apartment building and spoke in a heavy tone.

"Lead the way, ma'am."

2

SCARLET

I HAD A FEELING THAT DAMIEN CAME FROM AN ESSENTIALLY rich family. From his attire to his car and his manner of speaking, I could only imagine the size of his house. I felt embarrassed as I stepped into my apartment building. The hallway was rather narrow, with dim lights shining above. The paint was basically chipping off of the walls. I didn't dare look behind me. I was almost afraid of what his reaction would be to the building. We headed toward the small narrow elevator at the end of the hallway. He was following close behind me as the metal doors slowly opened up. We had just gotten into the elevator when I pressed the fourth-floor button, I turned around to face him, and saw a rather rested, calm smile dancing upon his lips.

My eyes lingered on him. "I know it's not very fancy."

Before I could continue speaking, he cut me off right away. He leaned carefully against the mirror in the elevator with his gaze resting upon my face. "Believe me, it's a lovely place and I assume you're renting it all on your own?"

His words were unexpected to say the least.

I nodded as the elevator doors slowly opened up and I made my way out toward the hallway. Damien's kindness surprised me. He could have easily been pretentious about the place. Instead, he had made me feel a tinge of appreciation, something I wasn't accustomed to.

We stopped outside Apartment Number Six. My keys jiggled within the lock of the rather beat-up wooden door before finally the knob turned, and I pushed the door open.

My apartment wasn't exactly huge, we entered into the living room with a small couch against a rusty wall, a TV on the rack and a knitting kit Nana had left out on the coffee table. The kitchen was just behind the living room. It was more like just three marble slabs and a stove. Two bedrooms were on opposite sides of the living room giving much-needed space.

I looked around the place and knew that Nana had fallen asleep. I turned to face Damien and noticed he had already taken his heavy coat off his broad shoulders. He had placed it neatly by the couch, and I felt my heart skipping a beat when I noticed the first two buttons of his perfectly fitted white shirt had been undone. I gulped before I brought my gaze back to his eyes and spoke.

"Would you like some tea?"

My breath slowed when Damien took a step closer to me; there were mere inches between us. The smell of his cologne spread through me, making me breathe a little heavier.

He smirked. "How are you feeling?"

I knew he was messing with me. He probably noticed the way my legs had turned to jelly with the single step he had taken toward me. I knew I could not let him get away with messing with me. I decided to play around equally.

I made sure my eyes were fixed on his emerald green eyes as I slowly began to bite my bottom lip. He was much taller than me, and his body was practically hovering over me. My bottom lip remained between my teeth for ten seconds as I refused to break eye contact with him and watched as his gaze narrowed toward me. He took another step toward me. I tried to take a step back but felt the couch colliding with my body.

Damian raised his left hand toward me, my breath got heavier, and his skin made contact with mine. He gently touched my jaw tilting my head upwards to meet his eyes. I could see a sense of longing within him. His index finger reached my bottom lip, and he pressed against it.

His lips grazed my ears as he whispered, " Careful....you don't want to get burned do you?" His words caused goosebumps to rise upon my skin.

I gulped. Just before he came closer to me, I whispered, "I'm not really fazed by fire."

I knew that once the words had left my mouth, things would go sideways. It took him less than a second before he moved his hand to the back of my neck, and he pulled me closer to him instantly. I knew what was coming, but the feeling that came with it was completely unexpected. He pulled me even closer which I didn't know was possible. Finally, our lips collided. My eyes fell shut. I could feel it as he took my bottom lip between his own teeth, and gasped as my fingers grabbed onto his broad shoulders.

For a moment, it felt as if time had started to sway in the background, like everything else was fading away, and it was just me and him, the stranger who knew exactly how to play with fire.

After a few moments, he pulled away so I could catch

my breath. He looked over at me and rubbed my bottom lip with the tip of his thumb.

I was still catching my breath when he gestured between the two bedrooms and mumbled, "I'm guessing we should take this inside? Unless you prefer the couch of course?"

He was being perfectly cocky and flirty at the same time. I begged my heart to calm down. I felt it kept skipping beats here and there. I pointed toward the room behind him, and he didn't need any more direction. At first, I was going to follow him, but I was completely surprised when he instantly took a knee. I gasped. Before I knew it, he had already lifted me in his arms he pushed me closer to his body and I instantly wrapped my arms around the back of his neck, he leaned forward and placed a kiss on the side of my cheek.

"Hold tight..." he whispered.

I did as I was told. He pushed open the wooden door to my bedroom while still holding me. He treated me as if I was not heavy for him at all.

I had a feeling his confidence came with experience and age. He seemed to know exactly what he was doing.

As soon as we walked into the bedroom, his eyes fell upon the double bed in the middle of the room. He slammed the door shut with his foot. He didn't even give it a second look. Damien's grip tightened on me before carefully laying me on the bed. His body was now on top of me. His gaze rested upon me, and he noticed how I was breathing deeply. He reached down to kiss my lips. Just as he pulled away he spoke in a mere whisper. "Are you sure you're okay?"

A small smile appeared on my lips. I lifted myself a little and made sure my lips collided with his. He instantly pulled my body closer as he moved onto the bed. Before I knew it, he had taken charge and he fully pulled me into his lap. He tugged at the hem of my shirt, and as he pulled it over my head. His lips took a mere two-second break from mine before they were again in contact with mine. I gasped when he managed to undo my bra with just the movement of one hand. I was still in his lap as I started to move my hips, pressing down on him. His bulge was pretty visible through his grey work trousers. I felt shivers down my spine when he dropped me down on the bed once again, he pulled his shirt off of his body, and I was faced with his lean figure, abs, and a rather broad-toned chest. He pushed himself over me and my fingers dug into his back as I felt his member pressing me. A moan escaped my lips.

Damien definitely knew what he was doing.

I whispered over to him, "You know exactly what you're doing right?"

He smirked. "I have twice as much experience than you could imagine."

I figured he was referring to the fact that he was double my age.

The moment he bit down on the skin of my neck, I gripped him even tighter. Before I knew it I was breathing heavier. He looked me in the eyes, and I knew exactly what he was asking. I wrapped my arm around the back of his neck. I pulled him closer.

"You ready?" he whispered.

I nodded my head. He smiled at me as he leaned in. His lips crashed into mine, and I moved my head upwards and wrapped my legs around his lower body. He pushed himself inside me slowly, and I gripped him even tighter. I couldn't hold it in as the room was soon filled with the sound of my moans between the kisses he would leave upon my body.

His thrusts picked up pace over time, and my nails dug deeper and deeper into his back.

The sheets were a mess. By the time we were done, he fell to my side. He snuck his arm under me and before I knew it, I was in his arms. He looked around my bedroom, and his eyes landed on the several posters on my walls. He raised an eyebrow when his gaze met the typewriter sitting on my white-painted desk.

He lifted his right hand and pointed at the typewriter. "Interesting choice of decor?"

I smiled. I lifted my body upwards so I could come face to face with him. "It's not for decor, I'm actually a writer. Or I'm trying to be one but you know how it goes with all the competition and all."

I cut myself off. Before I could go on, my eyes landed on the knuckles of his right hand, and my heart instantly sank. I could see traces of crimson-red blood stuck to his skin. It was as if his skin had split open in several places. The memory flashed before my eyes. It was his right hand that had collided with the man's jaw at the bar. Damien noticed the look on my face and asked if I was okay. I instantly slipped my hand into his and gestured toward the dried-up blood on his knuckles as I spoke.

"Why didn't you tell me you were bleeding? Does it hurt? Are you okay?"

The questions came slipping from my mouth one after the other. He smiled as if he was completely unfazed by all of it. Damien slowly ran his fingers through my hair and spoke softly almost like he was dealing with a kid. "It's honestly nothing. I've dealt with way worse."

I shook my head in disbelief. Slowly, I pulled myself out of bed and hurried toward the kitchen. He remained in bed, wondering where I went.

As I walked back into the room with my first aid kit, Damien pulled his body upwards, and now he was resting upon the bed frame. I made a point to position myself in his lap, my body weight resting upon his legs as I took his hand into mine. He watched me, his eyes didn't even dare blink as I cleaned the dried-up blood lining his skin before I placed the band-aid around his knuckles. I looked up at him, and he was staring at me with a sense of affection lingering in his eyes.

I raised my eyebrows. "See, now you're all good."

I waited for a reply, but instead, he instantly pushed upwards and turned us around. My back landed on the mattress, and he was on top of me once again. He kissed my neck before he looked up at me and smiled. Goosebumps rose upon my body as he began to plant kisses from my neck down to my stomach, and he paused, his nails digging into my hips. He looked up at me and my heart skipped a beat just before he began to place kisses on clit. He whispered, "I guess it's my turn to be thankful."

The room was once again filled with the sounds of my moans.

So this is what it felt like to play with fire.

Just as I had stopped moaning, he pulled himself on the bed closer to my body, and I noticed how he watched me as my breath heaved up and down.

"You're really used to making people lose their breath around you?" I asked.

He turned to face me as he spoke in a low tone,

"To be very honest I don't usually do this. It never really sticks you know."

I felt a pinch in my heart at his words. I ignored them as I tilted my head upwards. "It doesn't always end this way does it?"

He seemed distant as the words fell from his mouth. "Someone always gets hurt so I figure it's better to stay away."

I wanted to ask him more about what he meant but he turned to pull my body closer to his and I had a feeling he no longer wanted to talk about it. So I just decided to remain silent as my body began to drift off to sleep.

3

SCARLET

SUNLIGHT FILTERED THROUGH THE THIN WHITE CURTAINS IN the small bedroom. Streaks of light gold fell over my eyes as I flinched at the sense of warmth coming in through the window to the left side of my bed. My eyelids began to flutter open slowly; it felt as if the events of last night were still buried in the back of my head when my eyes met with the same pale white ceiling in my room.

I turned to my left slowly, and suddenly, I felt cold. My eyes landed on the other side of my bed, the comforter was carefully draped over the sheets, and the pillow lay there almost as if no one had been there last night.

I sighed. I didn't know why a part of me was expecting myself to wake up next to him. Even though the rest of my brain kept telling me there was no way I would ever see him again.

My fingers gripped my comforter as I asked myself if the events of the past night did even happen. He had barely left a trace of himself. The only thing I could smell was the strong scent of his cologne lining my sheets.

"Rich people perfume," I whispered to myself as I finally gathered the courage to pull myself out of bed.

I walked into the bathroom connected to my bedroom. As I looked up at the small mirror hanging above the sink, my breath paused. My eyes landed on the dark purple-shaded bruises resting messily upon the skin of my neck, reaching down to my collarbones like he had been on a mission to decorate stars upon my skin in violet. I was about to run out of concealer soon because of these.

As I washed my face and allowed the water droplets to remain clinging to my skin, the memories of the night before came crashing back to me in bits causing shivers to run down my spine. The way his eyes would wander over my body, his grip on my thighs, and the feeling that would rush to my head and make me dizzy when his lips collided with mine. I tried to push the memories out of the way telling myself it was nothing but a one-night stand.

I made my way across my bedroom, and half of me hoped to find a clue left behind. There was a stranger in my bed, but there was nothing left of him. The only thing I could see was the medical kit by the edge of the bed. A small smile appeared on my lips when I remembered what had happened after I had cleaned the blood from his knuckles. The night was one I would never forget, even if I had to let go of the idea of ever meeting the man again.

There was a tradition every morning. I step out of my bedroom and welcome the smell of freshly baked cookies. My mug of coffee would be on the kitchen counter, and Nana would be sitting by the television cursing at some politician, waiting for me to come in so she could tell me all about how capitalism is ruining the country. I stepped out of my bedroom with an oversized hoodie that easily reached my knees. I was on a mission to hide the bruises lining my skin. A part of me didn't feel like getting confronted early in the morning about the stranger in my bed. It wasn't like he was ever returning, so the conversation would be pointless.

I faked a smile as I entered the living room. Nana was, as usual, sitting across the living room on the couch. Her eyes were fixed on the television. She had a cup of tea placed neatly on the coffee table before her. I went straight to the coffeepot to make a cup of coffee. She hadn't even noticed me yet.

It wasn't until I finally cleared my throat and spoke up in a rather low tone that she tilted her head toward me.

"How are you feeling Nana? Let me guess. The douche is back on the screen?"

I was referring to the white man with slicked-back blonde hair on the television screen talking about women's bodies and what they should or should not do. I noticed a faint smile on Nana's face. The woman was easily in her late seventies, she had white hair leading down to her lower back, and it would always be neatly styled into braids. Wrinkles had started to form on her forehead and the corners of her eyes, especially when she smiled. Her lips would often be chapped in the winters, and she would always forget the chapstick. Nana was the sweetest soul you would ever meet, but at the same time, she was brutally honest. You would not like to be on her bad side.

I walked across the living room and stopped just by the coffee table. My eyes lingered over the stack of bills on the edge of the table. I gulped, knowing very well that it was time I faced them. My attention was pulled away from the sheer weight of responsibility on my back by Nana as she spoke.

"How was the storm yesterday honey? Not too harsh on you?"

I sat across from her on the rather dusty couch. I tried my best not to think too much about the events that followed the storm.

Keeping a straight face, I said, "Uh...it wasn't that bad. I found a place to lay low for a bit before it was over."

I looked up, and I instantly saw a change in Nana's expression. Something was up.

She raised an eyebrow. "The gentleman from the morning. Will he be coming back?"

She seemed honest with her question, like she wanted to know. My cheeks flushed a light shade of pink as I looked away from her.

"I don't think so," I whispered.

She noticed the way my face dropped, and she reached forward. She placed her hand over mine. "You never know honey; he seemed like the type to stick around."

I had no idea what Nana meant by those words, and all I could think about was the encounter she must have had with him. What did he say to her? Nana was hard to crack when it came to men. She wanted to make sure I ended up with someone I wouldn't end up running from later in life.

I pushed the thoughts related to Damien out of my mind and focused my attention on the bills at the corner of the table.

I offered Nana an apologetic look. "Well he was nice and all but it's time to go back to reality now. By reality I mean I'm going to finally call up the rude woman from the office and see if I can get an extension on one of these bills."

She lifted her thumb, almost as if she felt sorry for me. "Oh, I despise that woman on the phone."

I nodded as I pressed my phone to my ear. Before I knew it, I was connected to a Karen on the other side. I offered her my customer number and asked as politely as I could for an extension. Silence fell for a moment over the phone line before she finally spoke, "Ma'am your bills were paid earlier this morning. You don't seem to have any due at this time."

For a moment, I felt like I was hearing things. I almost dropped the phone from my palm as I looked up at Nana in disbelief, I didn't know why she let me call the woman if she had already worked a miracle. For the first time in my life, I found myself thanking Karen. As soon as I placed the phone back in its place, I turned to Nana with disbelief written all over my face. "Nana, why didn't you tell me you paid them? And how did you even manage to do this?"

She smirked and held up both her hands at the same time. "Honey, it wasn't me, but maybe you should ask the gentleman from the morning. I ran into him rummaging through the bills in the morning."

I had no idea how he could have managed to pull that off. I was shocked, but Nana wasn't done yet. She gestured toward an envelope that had been placed next to the bills as she said, "You might wait to see that. It came in your name today."

I wasn't sure if I was even prepared for any more surprises. My heart was thumping within my chest as I ripped open the envelope and opened the letter inside.

"Corelli Enterprise Call for Interview"

My eyes gazed over the words, I knew I had applied to a lot of places looking for a job but I had no recollection of applying to one of the largest tech firms in the country. The letter was sitting before me. Nana's eyes were fixed on me waiting for the news. I could think about how this event happened later, but for now, I just wanted to see a smile on her face.

I turned the letter toward her slowly. "I just got offered

an interview at one of the largest companies in the country, Nana."

There it was. The smile I was waiting to see.

I had no idea who was working the miracles in my life or what was going on; but, every part of me was eternally grateful.

4

—————

SCARLET

A RATHER SLOW WEEK HAD PASSED SINCE THE LETTER HAD arrived on my doorstep and all I could think about was that I hadn't even applied for the job. Getting an interview at a place like Corelli Enterprise would be the final step in the entire process. I wondered if they had picked up my CV from somewhere. It would still not make any sense at all considering I had merely just worked front desk jobs ever since my graduation. My doubts would go numb at the sight of my Nana. She told me its fate, and the only thing I should be focused on now is giving a good interview.

I would be lying if I said I hadn't spent most of my nights and days thinking about Damien, the handsome stranger who had stumbled inside my bed and disappeared the next morning. Every part of me wanted to stalk him on social media and find out exactly who he was, but of course, I had an internet bill that was long overdue, and even though it had been paid, the line wouldn't be connected until a week later.

Monday morning felt like it started with anxiety pouring through my body. I stared at myself in the mirror before me.

Sunlight filtered into the room through my rather thin satin curtains. I had decided to leave my blonde hair down since it reached my shoulders. Nana was pressing me about braids. Braids in her eyes would make me look "Neat" and "Professional." I barely had half a heart to tell her that no amount of braids would help the lack of experience within my resume. My expectations were low, to say the least.

I had thrown on a white button-up and paired it with what seemed to be a pencil skirt, perfume, and my clothes had been ironed three times over. A good impression was all that could save me is what I thought to myself as I heard the cab driver's voice pulling me away from my thoughts and back to reality.

"We're here Ma'am."

My eyes lingered out of the window. The sun was still out. We had driven out of the suburbs and into the main area of Crescent City. There was barely any traffic on the road. I couldn't even examine where he drove me,

"Ma'am we are here," he reminded me.

He probably wanted me to get out of his car. I handed him the cash, and slammed the back door of the taxi shut. I looked up, and I was face to face with one of the largest buildings I had come across in a while. Mirror glass was coating the entire building, designed in an ovary shape with large, white-painted gates at the front. I looked around, and my eyes fell upon the men walking by the gates in what looked to be security uniforms. I walked up to them, trying my best to keep my back straight as I secretly struggled with the heels on my feet.

One of the men in the uniforms asked what I was doing there, and I left not a second of silence between the two of us as I instantly whipped out the letter I had received from the company. He held the letter in his hands for a few moments as he read over it. I was surprised as the man called out to someone in the distance by the gate. A loud thud instantly filled the street, the white metal gates behind me began to open up, and I took a deep breath knowing very well that it was time to go in.

The man by the gate gestured to the huge driveway inside, speaking in a rather thick southern accent. "Alright, just follow the path and enter from the first door you see on the right."

I nodded as I headed inside the building. The path was set out in red bricks, and along both sides were what looked to be gardens layered heavily with flowers. I could hear my heels clicking against the path as I looked to my right. Beyond the entrance was a parking lot extending out toward the other side of the land. I still couldn't believe they had managed to make something like this in Northern California. I pulled myself out of my thoughts as I ran my fingers through my hair one last time before stepping in front of the automatic sliding door.

As soon as the double doors opened before me, I was met with a sudden cold breeze. Shivers ran down my spine. The building was twice as lavish on the inside. My eyes gazed over the whole space, the white-painted ceilings were so high my eyes barely could see them, and glass windows had the gardens outside on display. A large fountain painted in white was placed in the middle of the huge entrance, and my heels clicked over and over against marble-coated tiles filled with designs embedded in them.

I walked to my right where there was what seemed to be a huge reception desk. I stared at the woman who was seated behind the desk. She had bleached blonde hair tightly pulled into a ponytail. Her eyes were glued to the screen and I could see the lip fillers she had from a mile away. As I approached the desk, I stood there for a few seconds hoping she would notice me but she just kept scrolling through the screen in front of her.

I cleared my throat and maintained a fake smile. "Um...excuse me. I just wanted to ask where you're holding the interviews?"

I wasn't done speaking, but I was cut off in an instant. I caught the blonde woman's attention briefly before she flipped her head toward the entrance of the building. It seemed as if, at the moment, time had taken a pause. The sound of heels brutally collided against the marble floor. I twisted my head around immediately and noticed how everyone in the hall stopped what they were doing. It was as if they were all frozen in place. The double doors leading to the hall opened up, and the clicking of heels in the distance became louder. Soon enough, a woman's voice filled the area. It was rather shrill, the sound of a voice that bites at your earlobes and makes you pay attention without your will.

I watched from the corner by the reception desk as a woman with streaks of hazel in her hair practically burst into the hall. An iPad was resting on her arm. She flicked her rather long ponytail of hair extending down to her lower back toward the left as she turned back to the door. It seemed as if she was waiting for someone, but the person still hadn't reached her yet. The woman still spoke up again with a shrill tone.

"I don't understand how many times I can reschedule this. You do know that this is not a game right?"

She had now carefully placed her right hand upon her hip, wearing a tight skirt reaching barely down to her knees as her eyes remained fixed on the door. In just moments, the unexpected happened. Out of nowhere, I felt as if my breath was caught in my throat. Through the revolving double doors stepped a gentleman who seemed hauntingly familiar. Dark salt and pepper hair, diamond coated wristwatch, and a sleek winter coat on broad shoulders. My mouth fell open.

Damian walked through the door. Every single person in the whole hallway had their eyes on him. I wondered if they were just as surprised as me because he had never made an appearance here. The question hung in my mind. I watched as he walked closer to the woman in the skirt and spoke softly and calmly.

"Tory, I appreciate the effort but I am not interested in the brand deal. I believe we put an end to this conversation. On the other hand, I am waiting on the contracts from..."

He stopped in the middle of his sentence. He had finally looked up from the cell phone in his hand, and at that moment, his eyes met with mine.

Emerald Green.

I gulped, and he stopped speaking. The room refused to fall back into its natural pattern. He remained fixed on me. I could feel my legs going numb at the moment. Memories of the night I had dug my nails into his back came rushing back to me, and I gulped instantly. After a few short seconds, he cleared his throat. The girl in front of him with the IPad was about to say something, but she was cut off as Damien began to make his way past the fountain and across the huge hall. I realized instantly that he was indeed walking toward me. He swiftly slipped both his hands into the pockets of his winter coat. He didn't seem to be bothered by the stares he was getting from all of the workers in the hall.

The girl's voice echoed behind him as she followed. "What were you saying about the contract?"

She didn't receive a reply as Damien seemed bent on making his way past the multiple workers who offered him greetings, and he nodded to them with a faint smile. I remained still in my place. I knew that he was inches away from me when the smell of his strong cologne hit me. I took a step back. I watched as he barely even acknowledged me.

He leaned over the large reception desk and spoke to the blonde woman by the computer. "Anna you don't need to call Mr. Ronnie down, I can deal with this one."

My breath paused, the blonde woman's eyes flickered toward me, and I realized that I was truly "the one" they were talking about.

The blonde woman looked rather surprised as she spoke in a shaky tone. "Are you sure, Sir?"

He nodded firmly, and it seemed as if she understood. The woman in the skirt and the loud heels seemed bothered as she approached Damien with a rather tired look. "Really? So you won't take the time to read their contract but you have time for interviews?"

Damien turned around, his back was now facing me. I stayed still as he spoke, "Can you make sure the meeting room on five is empty? You can escort her there."

With that, he walked off toward a hallway extending toward the right. It seemed as if everyone in the room took a deep breath as soon as he was gone. The woman I assumed to be named Tory practically slammed her iPad onto the reception desk before she turned to me. Her expression seemed to turn soft as soon as her eyes landed on me and she spoke up.

"Could you please follow me?"

I nodded my head trying to be as polite as possible. As soon as we made it into a narrow hallway leading to the elevator, she tilted her head toward me as she said, "Don't mind him. Damien has a knack for doing exactly what he wants, whenever he wants to."

She rolled her eyes, and I assumed she was close to him. I was not afraid to ask, but by the time I realized I might be prying, the question had already left my mouth. "I'm sorry but who exactly is he?"

The elevator doors opened before us, and Tory's eyes widened at my question. She pressed the button to the fifth floor before a small smile escaped her lips. "You didn't come prepared did you?" I felt a sense of embarrassment warming up my body but before I had the chance to say anything she continued, "Damien is the CEO of Corelli Enterprise. He holds almost all shares of the company and he also happens to be very stubborn. I mean what's the point of having an advisor if you will never take their advice."

I felt as if it had gotten personal by the end. I stayed quiet as I began to piece together that the whole room had acted like they had seen a celebrity when he walked in. The elevator doors opened, and I followed Tory down another dimly lit hallway.

She stopped a few feet from wooden double doors and smiled at me. She gestured toward the doors. "Alright, good luck and don't take him too seriously. He's not half as intimidating as he seems."

I smiled. "Thanks." With that, she walked down the hallway.

I was there staring at the large wooden doors knowing exactly who was behind them.

My mystery man.

5

DAMIEN

THE AIR IN THE LARGE MEETING ROOM WAS RATHER CHILLY AND unpleasant. I took a deep breath as I slowly made my way toward the large wooden table in the center. To my right was a wall-sized screen where teams often presented their strategies to others. On the left side of the meeting room were desks with wall-sized windows overlooking Crescent City. It was nothing special. We didn't have a skyline or city lights glistening in the distance. My days at the New York Headquarters came back to my mind. We owned a building reaching the highest of heights in the city.

As I slowly began to drift toward the memories of the city I was suddenly pulled out of my thoughts by a soft knock on the door, I would not have heard it if I wasn't such an observant person when it came to my surroundings. I looked toward the door and sighed before speaking up while remaining in my seat on the furthest edge of the meeting table.

"Come in."

My fingers ran through my hair. I knew exactly who was on the other side of the door. The woman I could not get out of my head. I couldn't remember the last time I had driven anyone home myself let alone cut my schedule short just to conduct an interview personally.

My eyes drifted toward the double doors as they swiftly opened. From behind them, I caught a glimpse of light blonde hair. I smiled to myself when I noticed that she hadn't bothered to tie her hair up. She had allowed it to fall over her shoulders, and the gesture spoke volumes to me as someone who was tired of seeing the same ponytails and braids in and out of my offices across the country.

She seemed nervous. She was fiddling with what looked like an IPad which I assumed contained her resume. The woman stepped through the meeting room and instantly looked around. I watched as she gulped momentarily when her eyes landed on me. I politely gestured her toward the seat in front of me, and she walked over to the table allowing the clicking sounds of her heels against the tiles to echo in the meeting room.

As she took a seat a few meters away from me, I was instantly met with the smell of jasmine filling the air. I cleared my throat, our eyes met for a mere second in time, and I remembered them just the same. They had been stuck like a painting in the back of my mind.

Honey-coated deep brown.

She was the first to speak and I was half-glad at the fact. "So someone managed to pay all my bills a week ago. Would you know anything about that?"

I maintained eye contact with her as I shifted forward slowly in my seat making her nervous. And I would be lying if I said I wasn't used to making people feel a certain jittery way around me.

"Must be a gentleman who paid them. It's a shame. I have no idea who it could be."

She shifted around in her seat before speaking. "Truly is a shame. I would have loved to thank them personally."

I admired the way she could play around with words and bounce back to my sarcasm. I smiled before I pointed toward her Ipad on the meeting table as I spoke.

"May I?"

She instantly moved forward, and just as she was about to reach the file, her forearm collided with a glass of water on the edge of the meeting table. I saw it coming before it even happened. The crashing sound of the glass echoed in the room. I remained steady as shards of thick glass flew across the floor. I watched as Scarlet panicked right away. A small scream escaped her mouth, and her eyes widened to the point where I was worried her eyeballs might fall out. She looked at me, and I watched as guilt flashed across her eyes. She spoke up.

"Oh my God, I'm so sorry. Let me just deal with...."

Before she could go on, I noticed she had reached forward to pick up the broken glass. I moved from my seat right away and grabbed onto her arm. She tilted her head back and now her wide eyes were staring directly back at me.

I sighed as I gestured toward the broken glass. "Don't worry about it."

Before I could go on, I realized that I was still hanging on to her arm. I could practically see the way her chest was heaving up and down and her eyes were darting back and forth between the broken glass and me.

I decided to slowly let go of her arm, I lowered my tone as I moved my chair closer to her and whispered to her in the softest tone possible. "Hey, look at me. It's okay. Just focus on your breathing and forget about the glass. It's just a glass."

A few moments passed, and I could feel that she had finally started to calm down. She looked up at me and spoke in such a low tone that I barely even heard her. "I'm so sorry I didn't see the glass over there."

She trailed off, and I could practically see the guilt on her face. I didn't know what had gotten into me as I slowly lifted my hand and placed it upon her right hand, which was resting on the table. She looked up at me, and she was surprised by the sudden gesture. I spoke up, making sure my tone was still soft.

"You never have to apologize to me for being human. Remember that."

She nodded at me. I could tell that her breathing had calmed down now. A small smile spread across her face. When I saw that smile I felt a wave of relief. I noticed that she had looked down and was now staring at my hand which was still on top of hers. I cleared my throat as a sense of embarrassment washed over my body. I hadn't remembered the last time I had gone so far out of my way to ensure someone was alright. I slowly pulled my hand away from hers, and she shifted back in her chair. The tension between us had started to boil in the small, enclosed space.

I decided to cut the silence spreading in the room by pointing once again at her Ipad in front of us on the table. "Shall we?"

She was also pulled out of the trance we were both in. She found her resume, opened it, and carefully handed the Ipad to me.

I couldn't believe it! I was amazed! I was met with a rather remarkable presentation of more than just her resume. I raised my eyebrows in surprise, and she noticed as she spoke up immediately.

"If you think my lack of experience is funny, I'm right

there with you. I don't even know why you called me for the interview. I understand if you do not want to..."

Before she could go on rambling with a sense of panic, I cut her off. "I'm not smiling at your lack of experience, Scarlet. I am actually quite surprised that you managed to bring more than just the traditional electronic resume. I mostly have people coming to a tech company interview with a physical file containing everything I already know about them."

Her eyes widened right away. I realized I enjoyed watching the way her emotions would be on display in her expressions. She placed both her hands on the table, and her shoulders slumped down as she spoke in a witty tone. "Well, I may lack experience but I do need this job you know to pay bills and take care of Nana. I'm sure some stranger paying them for me was a one-time thing."

I smiled at her confidence and level of honesty.

She looked slightly devastated. She held on to the Ipad and looked over at me. "Well, I think I should stop taking up your precious time. I'm sorry about the glass and I think I will forever be grateful for everything that you have done for me. I had a feeling that I stood no chance but my Grandma, she's bent on believing in fate or whatever."

She rolled her eyes, and I stood beside her. "Your Grandma seems like a lovely woman, maybe you should take her up on the fate sermon."

She laughed as she shook her head and replied,

"Oh, come on please don't tell me you believe in it too?"

I looked away from her as the words left my mouth. "Ms. Hayes, you've been hired at Corelli Enterprise. I will send you a contract for hire asap. I hope to see the best from you."

Before I knew it, she shrieked. To my surprise, she jumped forward, and her arms were soon wrapped around the back of my neck. I was taken back by the sudden hug. I moved my hands toward her lower back and slowly pulled her body toward me. I could practically sense the huge smile on her face. Before any of us could say anything, a sudden crash sound filled our ears. I knew all too well what was happening, and at the moment, all I could think about was the girl in my arms. I knew I needed to protect her at all costs.

My heart skipped a beat, and the sound of glass shattering came from behind me. I grabbed onto her even tighter as all my fears began to turn into reality. I pushed her body down, making sure we were both covered and pulling her closer to me as I moved my back against the table. She had started to shake, and the loud sounds of crashing glass started to get worse in the distance. I tried my best to keep her body pressed to mine as we hid under the wooden meeting desk.

Scarlet screamed. The wall-sized window behind us collapsed and I knew immediately.

Bullets.

It was another attack.

6

SCARLET

I stood next to Damien, and suddenly, I was met with an instant clash of loud sounds, almost like thunder. The crashing sounds caused my body to freeze up instantly. I looked up and my eyes met Damien's. I saw the fear flashing within his own eyes and my heart skipped a beat.

Before I knew it, another large crash sound filled my ears. Damien moved forward and grabbed me by the arm. His grip was tight. It was almost as if he was afraid of letting me go. My body was pressed firmly against his and as I looked over his shoulder. The unexpected happened. I watched what seemed like bullets of rain flood through the huge wall-sized windows in the meeting room. I gripped on tighter to Damien's body as the glass shattered before my eyes. Shards of sharp glass spread across the room. Within seconds each window came crashing down, and a scream escaped from my mouth. Before I could focus more on where the bullets were coming from my body was suddenly pushed toward the large wooden table behind me.

Damian yanked my body as close to his as he possibly

could. I could practically feel my heart thumping out of my chest. Anxiety rose in my body. He was still gripping onto me. The bullets had now started to go through the open space where the windows once were. We were completely not protected. Damien grasped onto me and pulled me closer to him. He made sure his back was now facing the open area where the bullets were coming from, one after the other. I was practically shaking. He had pulled me under the wooden table as he pulled himself in front of me, I was gripping his white button-up, and I was moments away from squeezing my eyes shut. A part of me had believed that we were not going to survive what was going on. My hands were curved into fists as I held on to him for dear life.

My ears were ringing as the sounds of bullets colliding with the open wall got louder by the second. Damien held my body close to his. He must have noticed how I was practically shaking. He moved closer and whispered in my ear,

"Hey, it's going to be okay. I need you to stay with me, don't close your eyes Scarlet. I'm going to get you out of here. I promise."

In the moment the promise wasn't doing much for me. I was afraid deep on the inside, his promise had flicked a switch inside of me, and the trauma of my past relationships had started to get to me. I thought about all the times the man I thought I had fallen in love with gave me nothing but empty promises. I hoped deep down that Damien was different, but in a situation like this, I was concerned that if he didn't keep up with his promise, I would be stranded in a life-threatening situation all by myself.

I decided to focus on the ground as I tried my best to keep my eyes open. I could see pieces of broken glass laying on the marble floor. Damien yanked at my arm as he slowly pointed toward the door and spoke once again. "Let's head toward the door. Slowly, and keep yourself hidden under the table, okay?"

It almost felt like he was asking me if I could manage moving when dozens of bullets attacked the whole floor. I looked up at him and noticed that he had moved out from under the table as he took my hand and slowly began to move toward the door.

I panicked as I spoke up, suddenly stopping him in his way. "Wait, you're not covered, you'll get hurt!"

He shook his head as he gripped my hand tighter and spoke, "Don't worry about me right now we just have to focus on getting out of here..."

He was suddenly cut off by a bullet passing inches away from his body. I watched as it collided with the edge of the wooden table and a scream instantly escaped from my mouth. He ducked down low and moved onto his knees. I could see his body resting upon broken shards of glass on the ground and I flinched.

Before I could say anything, both of us turned toward the main door of the meeting hall. The door was practically busted open with a loud thud and soon my eyes landed on what looked to be a swat team dressed heavily in protective gear. Even with the team busting into the hall, the bullets did not stop raining inside the open space. I was still fixed on the men bearing heavy guns and bullet proof vests. Their faces were not visible under the protective masks on their heads. I was pulled out of my trance as my chest heaved up and down and panic settled in my stomach. Damien gripped onto me tighter as he spoke.

"On the count of three we're going to get up and run toward the door."

I turned my head toward the door and it seemed miles away. Tears were brimming in my eyes as I turned to Damien, and I shook my head as I spoke. "I....I can't Damien. I don't think I can do that."

He turned to face me as he spoke in a gentle tone. "Trust me, can you do that Scarlet? Can you trust me?" My surroundings had started to blur out in the distance. I could sense that the SWAT team began to circle us as he lifted my head by placing his hands gently under my chin before he spoke.

I knew that nothing made sense. If we stayed in the room any longer, we had no chance of getting out. He offered me his hand gently. I looked up and his eyes met mine. I tried my best to fight my tears as I nodded my head and just then he pushed my body upwards by yanking me with my arm. He pulled me to my feet. Without another second to waste, he began to run, his hand was still held in mine. I could see smoke lifting upwards in the background as I ran after him.

As soon as we rushed through the door, Damien's body collided with the wall in the hallway across the door. I didn't know what was going on. I followed him. My hand was still held in his as I watched him. His back was now against the wall. Sirens could be heard in the distance. It was almost as if I was slowly fading in and out of reality.

I looked down, and I noticed that Damian's face had gone pale. In the moment, I had no idea what had gotten into me but the anxiety seemed to wear off. My eyes drifted toward Damian's lower abdomen and they widened right away.

I could see crimson-red blood staining his white button-up. He pressed his palm against the wall and I noticed he was having trouble standing up. I pulled my hand away from him and decided to take charge of the situation even though my brain had no idea what was happening around me.

He tilted his head upward avoiding eye contact with me as I spoke.

"You got shot didn't you?"

He shook his head, but I could practically see the pain in his eyes. I ran my fingers over his lower abdomen and he reached for my hand. At the moment, I looked around for help but almost every single person from the rescue team was focused on putting out a fire in the meeting room. I knew I needed to do something to stop him from bleeding I couldn't let him just bleed out in front of me.

He watched as I slowly removed the black jacket from my back. He looked over at me in surprise. "Scarlet, what are you doing?"

I rolled my eyes at him as I began to unbutton his white shirt which was now pretty much stained with deep red at the bottom. He watched me as he flinched when I pulled his shirt over his broad shoulders. I could see what looked to be a gush of blood on his skin. It looked like a bullet had grazed him. I pressed my jacket tightly onto the wound, and as soon as I did, he grabbed onto my shoulder as tight as he could. He bit his bottom lip and I knew he was holding in a scream. I looked up at him, and tried to keep him calm as I spoke.

"Hey, just keep your eyes on me. I got you."

He smiled, and I could see dimples poking out from the sides of his cheeks. When he spoke, he flinched, and I could tell that it was hurting him even to talk. "You really keep getting in bloody situations with me don't you?"

I knew he was referring to the night he had hurt himself protecting me. I shook my head at him as I pressed onto his wound even tighter and he groaned out in pain. My jacket had started to drip with blood. I could tell that he needed proper medical attention and I couldn't keep the blood from leaking out of his body for any longer. I turned to my right and saw one of the team's men running toward us. Behind him was what looked to be a medical team. In the moment, I thanked God under my breath.

I turned to face the men with the medical kits. One of them looked over at me. Damien had his head facing the ceiling, and I could tell he was having trouble with the pain. His hand was still clasped in mine and pressing down on me.

The man spoke up as he looked down at the wound and then at me. "Ma'am you can step aside, we can take it from here."

I was about to step away from him when Damien grabbed on to my hand tighter as he spoke up in a mere whisper. His words were drowned in painful groans. "Please, stay."

He could barely get the words out of his mouth. I turned to look at the medics, and one of them slowly nodded his head. I could see a stretcher approaching in the distance. The men turned to me, and one of them slowly held his hand on top of the blood drenched jacket. As I let go, he gestured toward the stretcher and spoke in a low tone so only me and he could hear him.

"Let's pray to God it's not a bullet in there. Chances of survival are gonna run thin if that's the case."

His words hit me all at once, and I felt light-headed. But I knew if I displayed a reaction, Damien would get worried as well and so I decided to grab onto his hand with both of mine as I whispered over to him. "It's okay, you're going to be alright."

Deep down, a part of me feared I was about to lose him for good.

7

SCARLET

TIME PASSED BY ALMOST LIKE A BULLET TRAIN GOING THOUSANDS of miles per hour. I remembered flashes of everything. I found it odd when Damien's team refused to take him to the hospital. Instead, the ambulance was directly taken to what looked to be a mansion. He was in and out of sleep, but every time he opened his eyes, he checked for one thing: me to be by his side.

I was pulled out of my thoughts when I heard the doctor's voice in the distance. "He is stable. The bullet just grazed him. He got lucky."

I smiled at her. I sat in what looked to be an extremely fancy living room. I could see picture frames layered in gold and white rugs with marble-coated coffee tables. The same assistant, Tory, who had escorted me to the meeting room was sitting right next to me. Mascara had stained her cheeks as she fiddled with her thumbs. She stood up and began to speak to the doctor but in between the conversation, she turned to face me and spoke. "Honey, you can go in and see him now. I think he's awake."

I nodded my head and slowly got up. I walked across the

large hallway with decoration pieces lined against the walls. The wooden floors were polished and practically shining. I took a deep breath as I stood outside the freshly white-painted bedroom door. I knew Damien would be on the other side. I lifted my fist to knock on the door, but to my surprise, it just fell open.

I looked around, and I could see the large bedroom before me. A huge double bed was placed in the middle of the room. Opposite of the bed was a wall-sized screen and to the right was a window overlooking the city.

Damien's body was rested on the bed. He wasn't completely lying down; instead, his back was carefully lodged against the headboard with a couple of pillows behind him. Some strands of light grey hair fell over his forehead, and his eyes seemed tired. Wrinkles had started to form under his eyes. As soon as I entered through the door, his face lit up. He smiled at me, and the same dimples poked out from the sides of his cheeks.

I looked over at him, and couldn't help but mirror the same smile. Before I could even approach the bed, he said, "So I guess you can take credit for saving my ass huh?"

I shrugged as I sat down on the edge of the bed. "Oh please, I nearly passed out in the conference room when I heard the bullets. If you hadn't gotten me out of there I would have been..."

Before I could go on, Damien's hand gently fell upon mine. A sudden serious look took over his face as he read-justed himself in bed. The blanket slightly moved off his lower abdomen, and I could see a huge gauze wrapped around his lower body. I flinched, but my attention drifted back to him as he spoke up.

"I'm sorry that you ended up in that situation. It should

never have happened. I put your life in danger and I can't even begin to tell you how sorry I am."

I shook my head as I cut him off. "Tell me about the wound. You're the one who got shot. Are you okay now?"

He nodded. "Yeah it was just a slight graze. I have thin blood, so it looked bad; but trust me, I'm all patched up now."

I sighed as I looked at the gauze wrapped around his body and wondered if he was just pretending to be fine or if the pain was still there.

I couldn't help it. I had too many questions bubbling up inside of me. Before I knew it, the words already fell out of my mouth almost as if I had just blurted out what I was thinking.

"Damien, can I ask how you're just dealing with almost getting shot so calmly? I have not been able to think about anything but the moment in the meeting room since it happened and you're just acting as nothing happened?"

He shrugged. "I guess you missed the part about me where I served with US Marines for over twelve years of my life. My mind and body just adapted to chaotic situations and trust me, what you saw back there was minor. I have seen much worse in my time with the Marines."

It had all slowly started to make sense to me and I gasped. I had no idea that he had served as a Marine. This new information changed the way I had viewed him a lot.

The rest of the questions began to itch at me in the back of my mind even more now.

He squeezed my hand as he mumbled, "So you're not going to be suing Corelli Enterprise now, are you?"

He raised an eyebrow at me jokingly, and I fought back a smile. I knew what he was doing. He was using humor to deal with an otherwise horrifying incident. I shook my head and lowered my gaze while I thought more and more about exactly what had happened and how he was taking the whole situation. He must have noticed the sudden change in my expression because suddenly, I felt his grip tightening on my arm. I looked up with my eyes wide as he began to push me toward him on the bed.

I tilted my body sideways immediately, afraid of falling upon his wound. I had barely even gotten the chance to register that he had just pulled me almost on top of him when he instantly placed his hand under my chin, he lifted my head slowly and carefully until our eyes met, and whispered over to me gently. "Hey, you're going to be okay. I'm not going to let anything like that happen to you again."

I closed my eyes as soon as his lips collided with mine. He made sure to gently take my bottom lip within his teeth as his hands gripped my body tighter. Every part of me wanted to push him down against the bed and pull my body over him, but I was trying my hardest to be careful of his wound. He refused to let his lips move away from my body for a moment.

I tilted my head upwards as he kissed my neck. I groaned as soon he bit down on my neck and I grabbed onto his broad shoulders. My left hand was running through his hair, messing up the strands that were otherwise always perfectly styled.

He pulled his lips away from my body momentarily and I opened my eyes. His gaze was resting upon my face. He had a smirk on his lips as he gently tugged at the first two buttons of my shirt before he spoke.

"May I do the honors?"

There was something about his touch that made my head go a bit dizzy in the moment. I nodded my head slowly as I turned to face him, my eyes remaining on his body. He lifted himself upwards and I noticed that he flinched slightly as he unbuttoned my shirt slowly. He pushed it off my shoulders and slid his left hand under my back. Within seconds my bra was undone and tossed to the other side of the room. He placed kisses all over my body. As he reached the zipper of my skirt, he looked up at me before he whispered.

"I'm so glad nothing happened to you."

I felt my heart skipping a beat. I knew the doctor outside and Tory were about to hear a completely different side of me within seconds as soon as I heard the unzipping of his trousers.

The sun had already slowly started to set outside. My body was cuddled up next to Damien. He looked down on me and he smiled at the purple marks layered on my body. I felt my cheeks burning up. He gestured toward the gauze on his body as he spoke. "I think I wasn't too bad despite being injured."

He was referring to just how much he had made me moan within the last two hours. I was about to say something when we were both pulled out of our thoughts at the sound of a knock on the door. We both looked up, and I felt panic spreading through my body.

Damien placed his hand over mine. "It's just the chefs."

I nodded. My hands had almost been swallowed into the button-up Damien had given me to put on. It smelt of strong cologne and it had been perfectly ironed. It reached down to my knees.

"Come in," he called out.

Soon the door opened up, and what looked to be wooden-coated trolleys of food were brought into the room. The smell of food spread in the air and I realized just how hungry I had been the entire time.

The men in white uniforms placed the trolleys just near the bed. Tables were set just in arms reach of the two of us and they began to dress the tables with food. Damien gave the chefs a nod of approval. One of the men in white looked to be in his late fifties. He turned to Damien and smiled as he spoke,

"Wishing you a fast recovery, Sir."

"Thanks," Damian said before the man walked out of the room.

As soon as the door closed, it was just the two of us again. Damien carefully pulled himself upwards from the bed. He gestured toward the food on the table. I was about to follow him and get up when he said, "Wait, you stay there Ma'am. I will bring you whatever you need."

I laughed at the way he was treating me like I was royalty. I remained in the bed with my back against the bed frame as Damien picked up a plate. My eyes widened as he began to add rolls of sushi on my plate paired with ramen noodles and what looked to be oysters.

The words escaped my mouth out of surprise. "You're telling me your chefs made sushi?!"

He looked over at me and nodded like it was a random Tuesday morning for him and nothing special as he brought the plate over to me. I had no idea how this was all so casual to him. I would be okay with just mac and cheese from the box for an evening dinner.

He added the same kind of food on his plate and sat on one of the leather seats facing the couch. Before I took a bite of the food, my eyes landed on the gauze wrapped around his lower body, and instantly, something sparked inside me.

"Damien, can I ask you something?" I blurted out, without giving myself time to think.

He looked up from his plate. He put down his fork carefully as he nodded. All of his attention was now directly falling on me.

I cleared my throat. "Do you know why we got attacked at the office? I mean it seems like you've been through something like this before. Were they targeting you Damien?"

I watched as his expression suddenly changed. My heart skipped a beat. I knew he had trouble opening up so I decided to be the first to open up a little just to show him that it was okay for him to trust me.

"Damien, I think I have a right to know. I mean, we almost got killed and I don't even know what for. I haven't really told anyone this about myself but I was with someone who would keep secrets from me all the time about his business, his family, and come to find out other women. I am tired of being in the dark. Please just open up to me. I think I deserve your full honesty at this point!"

His eyes fell away from mine like he was trying to avoid me.

He spoke up in a rather robotic manner. "It's nothing for you to stress about Scarlet, as I said I will never allow for you to be in a position like this again."

I felt a sense of sudden offense taking over my body. I placed the plate of food to the side, raised my eyebrow at him, and said, "Wait so you know who did it but you don't trust me enough to tell me anything right?"

He shook his head as I waited for him to open up finally. But instead, what he said next just disappointed me further. "It's not about trust Scarlet. I just can't get into this right now. It's a long story and frankly, it doesn't matter. I'm taking care of the situation as we speak."

I watched as the anger was visible on his face. I could tell that he was getting mad at me but I didn't care. I wanted to know the truth at all costs.

"Damien, I just opened up to you. I told you I don't want to be with someone who keeps secrets from me. All I am asking is for you to tell me why I almost lost my life and so did you?"

He practically slammed his plate on the glass coffee table beside him. He sighed loudly. He even refused to look at me. "I am going to tell you everything but with time. Can we please not do this right now? You're pushing me to..."

I noticed that I had never seen this side of him before. I had never seen him this angry. I cut him off before he could go on. "I'm pushing you to do what? Are you going to yell at me now just because I asked for the truth? Is this how it's going to be?"

He was about to say something else, but I felt anger burning in my body.

I stood up and began to put on my pants that were lying at the edge of the bed. He stood up as soon as he saw me, and spoke up instantly while he was walking toward me. "Scarlet wait. Come on. At least eat something. We can talk about this later."

I shook my head as I grabbed my bag from the corner of the bed and headed toward the door. Damien rushed after me, he tried to grab onto my hand, but I quickly pushed it away. Just as my palm rested on the doorknob of the bedroom door, I turned to face him. "You can come talk to me when you trust me enough to give me the truth. Until then please stay away from me."

I didn't stare at him any longer as I made my way out of the bedroom with anger and hurt burning through my chest.

8

DAMIEN

As soon as she had stepped outside, I felt like my heart had sank. I didn't know if I had been too harsh with her. I was just trying to protect her from all the darkness in my life. The one thing I felt good about was the fact that now I made sure security was watching us both at all times. I knew I needed her. She was the only person who made me feel like I was more than just some money-obsessed bachelor refusing to settle down again in my late forties. She brought out a part of me I thought I had lost. And deep down, I knew she needed me. The job would set her up for life. My protection and the comfort I had to provide her were essentially part of what she needed from me. Apart from the feelings that had sparked between us, I knew that our relationship had a lot more riding on it.

As soon as I made my way out of the house, I felt as if I could finally breathe. I took a moment to stand by the sidewalk leading to a small street filled with cafes and Christmas lights in the distance.

I barely stepped toward the sidewalk when my eyes landed on her. There she was. It looked like her eyes were equally focused on the street lit up ahead. I took a step toward her. Scarlet's back was turned to me.

"Come here. You're probably freezing out here," I said, gently.

She turned around, and for a moment, she just froze. I assumed she was really not expecting me.

She rolled her eyes. "Are you finally ready to open up?"

I offered her a kind and genuine smile before I gestured toward the black-colored jacket I had grabbed for her on my way out knowing she was freezing without one on.

"At least put this on first. You're probably shivering."

She nodded in annoyance as I approached her slowly and placed the jacket on her shoulders. She pulled it closer to her. "Thanks," she whispered.

I slid my hand into hers, and Scarlet looked over at me. Our eyes met in a mere moment. "How about some coffee? I know a really great place down here."

I pointed toward the street filled with lights and beautifully lined cafes. I figured if we had to talk, we could do it somewhere she could learn a bit more about me.

She looked over at me and I could see a spark in her eyes. It caused my heart to skip a beat.

We walked down the street toward the multiple cafes and my eyes caught sight of the beautiful Christmas decorations. The whole street was lined by colorful fairy lights glistening in the distance, and a smile immediately spread across my face. Children were running around with their parents chasing after them, and the smell of coffee filled the air. Christmas trees were put up with colorful bells hanging from them. My hand remained held in hers.

I stopped in the middle of the cobblestone street and pointed toward a small cafe to our right. "I have religiously been going here for the coffee almost every time I need a moment to think for myself," I said.

I hadn't really ever invited someone to a spot I considered to be for my own solitude but, at the moment, I felt I was more prepared to let her in than I had been with anyone else.

I had a feeling Scarlet had noticed that this was also my effort to open up to her. She squeezed her hand in mine and pointed toward the cafe as she spoke in awe.

"It looks lovely."

I began to drag her toward the coffee shop with a light red painted door at the front. She followed me as I pushed the door open, and we stumbled inside.

My eyes looked over the small place. Yellow fairy lights were spread around a small Christmas tree at the entrance, and the counter to my right had been filled with what looked to be freshly baked goods. As soon as we stumbled inside the woman behind the counter, Martha who was easily in her late sixties, turned to face us. Her eyes lit up immediately.

I waved at her politely, and she spoke from behind the counter. "Ah, isn't it lovely to see you again, and who must the beautiful lady be?"

She gestured toward Scarlet, and I offered her a kind smile and said, "Martha, I truly missed you. Scarlet this is Martha. She's the owner and she personally bakes all the marvelous cookies here."

I reached forward and shook the woman's hand. She seemed delighted to see me. She pointed toward a table for two by the window on the left. "Why don't you two love birds take a seat and, Damien, I'll bring your usual order right to you."

I instantly let out a little laugh at the choice of her

words. Scarlet's cheeks flushed pink when she heard what the woman had said as she followed me toward the small table. As soon as we both sat down, I grabbed her hand again.

I didn't waste a single second. "Scarlet, I'm sorry I didn't tell you everything right away."

All her attention was focused on me as she replied, "It's okay. You're here now, and I'm ready to listen."

I was glad she hadn't given up on me just yet.

I took a deep breath before I began to speak. "So the attacks started six months ago. At first, it was little things like sabotaging my company's strategies but then it started to get worse. You know the world of corporate is not what it seems from afar. Once you make it big, everyone needs a piece of cake. There was a shady company that wanted to work with us. They wanted the main plan we've been working on. I wanted to take my company toward hybrid cars, and they wanted to steal our designs."

I took a pause when I noticed that Martha had approached us again and placed two cups of coffee before us with a stack of freshly baked cookies. I smiled as she told us to enjoy ourselves.

I picked up where I left off. "I tried my best to handle the situation civilly but it didn't work and before I knew it a war had started. Things got personal very soon and even now I'm trying to control the situation. But this time the line has been crossed. They physically attacked my company and more importantly someone I care very much about."

I knew I had left out some details, but I was trying my best to paint a picture for her to see without confusing her too much. I just wanted her to know that I was doing everything in my power to protect her from my demons.

She picked up her cup of coffee and a moan escaped her

mouth as soon as she took a sip. I began to laugh as she nodded at me and her eyes widened in embarrassment. She covered her mouth as I endearingly stared at her.

I raised my eyebrows. "Yeah, that's the reaction I was waiting for."

She instantly smiled at me. I rubbed the top of her hand with my left thumb as she spoke, refusing to break eye contact with me.

"Thank you for telling me and opening up. I know it's hard for you and you have a lot at stake, but I just want you to know that I am not going anywhere. Even if it means keeping my life in danger, Damien. I'm choosing you."

Her words to me felt like a huge weight had just lifted off of my shoulders. "Don't worry. I promise to never let you down again. Right now my assistant Tory is working on your contract as my secretary. Before you know it, you'll be working for one of the best companies in the country."

Her eyes widened at me. She cleared her throat. "What exactly would I be doing as your secretary?"

I smiled. "You're going to be in charge of all my appointments and schedule. Apart from that, Tory will keep you updated if we need any other paperwork from you before you get started."

Before she had the chance to say anything at all I reached into the pocket of my heavy winter coat and pulled out a gold lined envelope with flowers engraved at the front.

I carefully slid the envelope across the table and toward her as I spoke. "I have to head back to the office and deal with the damage, but I told Karl to drop you off at home safely, and this is for you.'

Scarlet instantly reached for the envelope, and just as she was about to pull it open, I placed my hand over hers. I stopped her and said, "You can open it back at your place."

She stared at me with confusion written all over her face; but, I didn't give her a chance to complain as I split one of the chocolate chip cookies into two and offered her a bite.

As soon as she took a bite, her eyes widened, and I gave her a confident nod knowing she had just tasted a piece of heaven.

A few moments passed before I knew she needed to go check up on her Nana and I had to hurry back to the office.

I was the first to get up, and she followed me. We thanked Martha, and I turned to face her as soon as we stepped out of the cafe. I held both of my hands in hers as I carefully placed a kiss on her forehead and spoke in a gentle tone.

"You take care of yourself, okay? I had security placed around your apartment and ensured the best cuisine was delivered to your Nana's doorstep."

She smiled and thanked me. I shrugged my shoulders before I opened up the car door for her and before I knew it, she was gone.

As soon as I got into my car, my phone in the side pocket of my winter coat rung. I pulled it out. It was Tory. As soon as I placed the phone to my ear her voice came through. "Damien, I just wanted you to be aware that we have the final contract drafted for Scarlet."

There was a pause and I knew Tory well enough to know that bad news was coming so I went straight to the point. "I have a feeling there is a but coming."

She spoke up again, "The HR team isn't sure about hiring her. I haven't told anyone about your relationship yet, but Damien, as soon as you take her to the Masquerade Ball and make it public, you know she cannot work for you legally? A scandal is the last thing your company needs right now. I would advise you to keep this relationship of yours on the low, please, for your sake and hers."

I sighed. Deep down, I knew Tory was right. We couldn't have a relationship while I was her boss, but I had already invited her to the Ball.

I sighed. "Listen, she's not officially an employee yet. Let her go to the ball with me, and by the time she signs the contract, I'll keep it low, and the newspapers will forget and move on to the next big news. But for now, I need to show a united front. I need to show the people who attacked us that she is not someone they can mess with."

Tory just told me to be careful, and before I knew it, the line went silent.

IN THE DISTANCE across the street, a matte black car was parked not too far away from my own. I wondered if they were watching. I had a feeling I was always being watched and it wasn't going away soon.

9

SCARLET

"Nana you don't understand everyone is going to be there, like the press and the media and I just read in a newspaper that Damien has never gone to an event like this with a date!"

Nana smirked at me as she spoke, taking me off guard suddenly. "You know I always support you my love but what do you think about him putting your life at risk and being so much older than you? Are you okay with it? After the last man you dated, I thought you told me age was the problem with him too?"

I didn't like when Nana would bring up my old relationships.

I turned to face her. "I know the last one was older than me too but Nana he never treated me right from the start. And Damien is doing everything in his power to protect me. He literally risked his life for me a week ago and he will stop the bad guys. You just watch. Not to mention the fact that I need this job more than anything, he cares for me, and with this new contract that will soon be made, we can finally get out of this place and go live somewhere nice. We won't have

57

to worry about the bills being overdue, which especially stresses you out too much with your current health situation. And I will have time to focus on my love for writing."

The panic was spreading through my voice as I tried to show her my perspective of the relationship I had with Damien. Nana was standing in front of me, staring at the open envelope that Damien had handed me. She placed her hand on her left hip as she watched me panic in the distance.

Damien had dropped a bomb upon me out of nowhere. When I opened the envelope, I learned that I had been invited to a Masquerade Ball as his date. However, this was not just any Masquerade Ball. This was the equivalent of the MET Gala for Celebrities and I had multiple reasons to panic. Not only had I never been to an event like this in the public eye but I also did not have anything to wear to the event. The ball had completely slipped my mind with everything going on including one of Nana's health scares, and now it was the night of the event. I had completely flipped my closet upside down looking for something to wear since I had not told Damien because I didn't want to give him something else to worry about and fix for me. He had enough going on.

Nana was trying her best to make me feel like I would be accepted, but I wasn't sure it would work out with the three dresses I had in my closet being more than a year old each. Nana moved forward and placed her hand on my shoulder as she spoke.

"Why don't you talk to Damien about this? He can tell you what to wear."

I shook my head. Just as I was about to tell her I didn't want to worry him both of our attention moved toward the main door of my apartment. A firm knock on the door and a smile spread across Nana's face. I ignored how she was smirking as I rushed toward the door. As soon as I pushed it open my eyes widened. Damien stood outside my door wearing a suit neatly draped over his body and a bow tie. The smell of his cologne had taken over the entire hallway.

I was shocked. "Wait, weren't you supposed to come pick me up in two hours?"

A smirk spread across his face, I looked down and noticed a huge black colored box in his hands. He handed it to me as he gently kissed my cheek and whispered. "I decided to bring you your present myself instead of just sending Karl."

I moved out of the way and he stepped inside the house. As soon as he made his way inside, his eyes landed on Nana. I had never seen Nana this way around a man I was dating. She practically placed both her arms around his body and hugged him despite her questioning him just moments before. Damien was just as equally involved in the hug as well.

Nana began to talk to him, and I decided to place the box on the couch. I slowly began to open it, and once I had placed the lid aside, my eyes met with what looked to be one of the most beautiful emerald green dresses I had ever seen before. I lifted it slowly as I gasped. It was a long dress, and I assumed it would reach down to my feet with a slit reaching up to the thigh from the left side. Diamonds were glistening upon the deep neckline of the dress, and I turned to face Damien in surprise.

A smile was placed on his lips as he saw my reaction. I turned back toward the box and saw a pair of heels in the same Emerald Green shade and a mask with jewels embroidered along the shape of the eyes.

He stared at me as he noticed my reaction and then finally asked, "So, do you like it?"

My mouth hung open as I tried to contain my excitement. Nana spoke first, "Of course she likes it! I haven't seen that light in her eyes since she was eleven and her father took her to New York."

I rolled my eyes at Nana as I walked toward Damien. I took him by surprise when I wrapped my arms around his shoulders and pulled him closer to my body as I whispered in his ear. "I love it. It's perfect."

He threw his hands in the air. "Tory deserves most of the credit in this situation since she was the one who told me that you would appreciate this dress."

I smiled at him. I was about to ask him to thank Tory for me but Damien decided to place both his hands on my shoulders as he began to push me toward my bedroom and he whispered in my ear, "We don't have time, let me talk politics with Nana while you get dressed, and don't take too long."

With the smirk on his face, I knew he didn't care about us being late. He just wanted to see me in the dress he bought.

I took a deep breath as I stared at myself in the mirror before me. My hair had been neatly pulled up in a small ponytail. The dress was neatly draped over my body perfectly hugging all my curves. For a moment, I couldn't even recognize the person in front of me. The emerald green dress had a slit going up to my thigh from the left side. My skin was glowing as I placed one foot forward and the heels he had bought me came on display. The diamond-coated straps were reaching up to my ankles and I could feel that I had grown almost a good three inches more.

I wasn't done looking at myself in the mirror yet when I

heard a loud knock on my bedroom door. I knew who it was already. "Come in," I whispered under my breath.

The door slowly opened up with a small creek. I turned around, and there he was in his ever-so-perfect tux. His jaw dropped open as soon as he saw me.

He cleared his throat, and when he spoke. I noticed that his voice cracked a little as he walked toward me. "I....I just wanted to tell you we should be heading out."

He approached me, and I could see his figure right behind me in the mirror. I smiled at him through the reflection. He lifted his left hand, and his fingers began to graze my skin slowly. He started with my hands, reaching up to my arms with the lightest of touch. He placed his chin upon my shoulder and slowly began kissing my neck. I knew exactly where this was going, so I turned around to face him, his hand drifting to his side, and I spoke up with a flirty tone.

"Shall we?"

I gestured toward the door, but he lifted his hand up, stopping me. "Give me a moment, let me take you in, you look absolutely delicious Scarlet."

The blood rushed to my cheeks in the moment as I decided to play a little game with him and I winked at him. Before he could do exactly what was going on in his mind, I rushed past him and toward the main door of the house. He followed me. I stopped in the hallway and my eyes landed on Nana. She had the brightest smile spread across her face.

She offered me a kiss as she blew it in the air. "You look splendid my love, have a blast and I better hear all the news on the Kardashian's when you get back."

I blew a kiss back at her. Damien hugged my Grandma before we both made our way down the hall toward the car waiting for us downstairs.

As soon as we got in the matte black Mercedes parked outside, Damien turned to me. There was a screen between the driver Karl and the backseat. My breath hitched as soon as Damien's hand gripped my thigh. I could sense the lust in his eyes. He grabbed my head as he pushed his body closer to mine and I felt his breath grazing my skin as he whispered over to me.

"So you like teasing me now huh?"

I gulped as I felt his grip tightening upon my thigh, I decided to take things another step ahead. I reached down to grab on to his hand and I began to move it upwards through the open split in my dress. Just as his fingers moved beyond my thighs I looked up at him and made sure we maintained eye contact before I bit down on my bottom lip. He instantly realized what was happening and a smirk spread across his face. He reached closer to my ear again as he spoke.

"Really? You're going to play with me by not wearing any panties?"

I shrugged and spoke in a completely innocent tone, "You should have thought of those when you were getting the dress."

He knew exactly what game I was playing but I didn't know what was coming next as the chess board was suddenly flipped on me.

He moved his body forward as he pushed me down. My head was resting upon the leather-coated interior of the car. His fingers reached for my clit. Just as he pushed two fingers inside of me his right hand reached for my neck. He pressed on my neck and my eyes remained fixed on him. He reached down and began to place kisses on my collarbone. Goosebumps rose upon my whole body. A moan escaped my lips, and he instantly kissed me while his hand pressed down on my neck. His fingers refused to move from inside me.

He reached for my ear as he whispered, "If you moan one more time you'll be getting out of here with my handprint on your ass. Better keep it quiet princess."

I felt a sudden sense of magnetism pulling him closer to me. The dominance in his tone made my heart skip a beat.

I had lost myself in his eyes. My body was shaking at his command, and time seemed to drift away. I hadn't even realized we had reached the Ball until Damien moved away from me. I was still out of breath. He ran his fingers along the side of my face before he kissed my forehead. The count of cameras flashing began to enter my ears from a distance.

He gave me his hand and helped me back up in the seat before he whispered, "I promise I will allow you to moan as much as you want once we get done here."

The anxiety was gone. The fear of stepping out before half of the world had subsided as soon as he placed his hand in mine. The windows were tinted. I took a deep breath as I heard the click of the car door opening. The flashes of the cameras could be heard in the distance, paparazzi were lined up behind the gates of the event, and I could already spot celebrities in the distance. Damien looked over to me with a smile on his face. I gripped his hand tighter as I spoke in a low tone.

"I guess everyone is going to know about us now."

He shrugged his shoulders as he smiled. "It's about time the world knows that you belong to me, and I to you."

Shivers ran down my spine. Time was running out. I could hear them chanting his name.

Just before I stepped out of the vehicle, Damian turned to me. "You ready?"

I nodded. "More than I ever will be."

10

SCARLET

The red carpet wasn't half as stressful as I had imagined it to be. Damien was with me the entire time and he refused to let go of my hand for even a second. Half of my anxiety had already left my body. The hard part was still left. I took a deep breath as we went up the huge stone stairway leading to an ancient building decorated with lights. Large gates with carvings were swung open for the guests. Just before we stepped inside, we pulled down our masks to cover our faces. I could hear classical music playing in the background, waiters walked around with champagne glasses, and everyone was in exquisite gowns.

Couples danced around. People stood together laughing. Damien turned to me and gently placed his hand on the small of my back. "See, I told you it wasn't going to be that bad."

My anxiety hadn't yet fully left my body. I rolled my eyes at him. "Oh please, it's not over yet."

He shrugged before one of the waiters stopped by us with a tray of champagne. He grabbed two glasses, and a laugh escaped my lips when he did a little bow before moving one of the glasses toward me and spoke in a fake British accent. "One for the Lady."

I took the glass and looked around. The event seemed like something straight out of a fairytale. The couple had their hands in each other's as the men swarmed their women around, and the clicking of heels was heard in the distance. The marble floors of the old building were glittering, there was a choir playing at the stage just beyond the dance floor, and everything seemed to be in a certain order. Damien had noticed how I was looking around, and he raised an eyebrow at me when he noticed that I looked disturbed.

"Is everything okay, love?" he asked.

My heart skipped a beat at his choice of words. I turned to him and spoke in a low tone. "A few years ago I dated a man who was pretty established and well-known as well."

Damien cut me off with a joke before I could go on. "Oh, so you seem to have a type do you?"

I shrugged his words away as I kept going. I gestured toward the grand party before I spoke. "He would make me many empty promises, he would tell me he would take me to all these fancy parties once the time was right but he just had a knack for keeping me hidden away from the world."

Damien placed our empty glasses of wine on the table to our right before he took my hand. "Well, you're here now with me and I promise to never make you feel hidden away."

Before I knew it, he whipped me toward the dance floor. I placed both my hands on his shoulders and he swayed with me from side to side. Anxiety rushed up my body, and he noticed. He reached for my hand and placed a kiss on my knuckles before he noticed the way I was staring at all the couples who were in perfect harmony with each other.

I was embarrassed as I spoke in a low and rather

defeated tone. "I don't really know how to do the dance. I'm sorry. I know I should have practiced before. I don't want to embarrass you Damien."

He seemed not to give a care in the world. He placed my hands back on his shoulders as he brought his body closer to mine until we were merely inches apart from each other. His right hand was perfectly placed on my lower back.

He moved forward and whispered in my ear. "It's a party Scarlet, we came here to have fun and be ourselves. Forget what everyone else is thinking and just do as you please. Trust me, there is no such thing as embarrassment when it comes to having fun and enjoying in your own element."

I nodded. He seemed to be the only person who could calm my intrusive thoughts. Before I knew what was going on Damien took my hand in his, he lifted his hand upwards and twirled my whole body around on the dance floor. A laugh escaped my lips. I couldn't remember the last time I was this happy. My heels clicked against the marble floors, and for a moment I had completely lost track of the fact that there was anyone at all around us. It was as if everyone else had faded away in the background, and it was just him and me. The music started to pick up its pace in the background, he continued to move my body along with his to the rhythm, and we danced as if no one was watching us.

Everything was going better than I had ever imagined it until Damien pushed my body backward intending to pull me back toward him. However, I stumbled and lost my balance. I felt my body falling backward and colliding with an older woman who seemed to be dancing with her husband. I turned around and instantly began to apologize without even thinking twice. Her husband reached forward and shook his head telling me it was all okay.

However, as soon as my eyes landed on the old woman,

my heart dropped for a moment. I couldn't see her whole face as a mask pretty much covered it but I could see that she had rolled her eyes at me as she turned to face her husband. I knew that maybe she did not mean for me to hear what she had said but her words were loud enough to reach me. They replayed in my head again and again, and I felt as if every insecurity I had ever had slowly began to crawl up the surface.

"You would think Damien is old enough to stop messing with these young gold diggers by now. She stepped on my shoe, one she couldn't buy it if she worked all her life."

I began to drift. The anxiety was up my chest. I couldn't breathe. Damien grabbed onto me from my waist, and as soon as he twisted me around, he noticed that something was off. I could feel the walls of my surroundings closing in on me and I could tell that he was saying something, but his words began to blend into the white noise around me.

I pushed his hands away from me before I excused myself and ran toward the hall leading to the bathrooms. I could hear his footsteps behind me but I just picked up my pace and made sure to move through the crowds of people coming toward me. I knew the crowd would slow him down as I rushed toward the large golden doors with the painted bathroom sign.

As soon as I stepped into the bathroom, the first thing I did was shrug the mask off of my face. I felt like I needed just to breathe. The woman's words came back to me once again and I didn't know how to react. A part of me felt ashamed telling Damien as I wondered what he would think of me.

I was so lost in my trance that I barely noticed as a woman next to me called out to me. "Honey, are you okay?"

"Oh you poor thing. Take deep breaths. You're going to be okay."

I looked to my left and my eyes landed on a blonde haired woman who looked to be easily around Damien's age. She smiled at me and wrinkles popped up around the corners of her eyes. She was wearing a navy blue colored mask filled with emeralds and a matching colored dress. I decided to focus on her eyes and slowly I could feel my breathing calming down.

Once I was more stable, I said, "Thank you."

She gently placed her hand over my shoulder. "You must be Damien's girlfriend. I'm sorry to startle you, but as soon as my eyes landed on your dress I just realized that you walked the red carpet with him, didn't you? Oh I must say you are beautiful."

The words came to me like a breath of fresh air.

She winked at me as she continued, "He's a lucky man you know."

"Thank you, but I think I am just as grateful for him," I said.

"Oh please, after the scandal he had when he impregnated and left his ex-wife? But I know Bella is the sweetest child. She takes just after her dad doesn't she?"

I froze.

I didn't know what she was talking about, and a look of horror spread across my face.

Did Damien have a child he had not told me about?"

As soon as the woman noticed the look on my face she stepped back. She looked just as horrified as she turned to me and spoke.

"Oh, my bad, I just assumed he would have introduced you to his daughter by now. Please forget I said anything and take care."

She stumbled out of the bathroom like someone had just stolen something from a corner store. She asked me to forget, but it felt like my whole world was collapsing.

I decided not to show emotions to the snobby people at the party as I headed toward the exit. I could hear Damien calling out to me. People I had never seen before were looking for me. I made sure to put my mask over my face as I hurried down the marble steps of the large building leaving the music and the people behind. My eyes landed on the same pitch-black Mercedes we came in and I instantly pulled the door open.

I had assumed Karl would approach me but as soon as I sat inside the car, it started moving. I rested my back against the car seat.

I spoke to Karl as we left the building. "Karl, can you do me a favor? Can you drop me by the bar on the corner street near my house? I don't feel like going home yet."

A few moments passed and I didn't hear anything back from him. It wasn't usually like this. Karl would respond instantly. I looked around the car, and suddenly, my heart skipped a beat. The seats of the car were painted in red leather, not black.

"This wasn't Damien's car."

My heartbeat sped up I reached for the door handle, but before I could do anything at all the separation between the driver's seat began to open up. I turned my head, and my eyes landed on a man. He was wearing gloves. He reached backward from the passenger seat, and before I knew it he gripped my mouth.

My head fell backward and everything around me began to blur out before I fell into complete darkness.

11

———

DAMIEN

I COULD FEEL MY HEART THUMPING AGAINST MY CHEST. AS I looked around the extravagant venue, my eyes searched for a certain woman in an emerald green dress, but I couldn't see her anywhere. I was right behind her but she had disappeared into the crowd, and I had no idea what even happened. I thought she would come back looking for me too. I tried my best to make her feel comfortable throughout the evening, but somewhere along the way something went wrong obviously. Now I had lost her.

I yelled into the phone before Karl could even say anything. "Karl we have a problem. I need you to send the team here right now. I can't find Scarlet and I've looked everywhere."

As soon as he said he was sending the team, I felt calmer. I was just about to head toward the exit when my eyes landed on one of the guards who was standing by the large metal gate at the exit. I ran toward him and pulled out my phone. The first news article my eyes landed on had a large picture of Scarlet and me on the red carpet.

I practically shoved the phone in the man's face as I

gestured toward the exit and spoke. "Have you seen this woman leaving the venue by any chance?"

To my surprise, the guard nodded his head yes. He glanced at his watch. "It's been approximately an hour and a half since I saw her leaving."

My heart dropped. There was no way she could have gone back home. The event had banned all public transport and taxi's. I was just on the phone with Karl, and he hadn't seen her either. The worst thoughts began to get to my head, but I had to calm myself down. I reached for my phone, and as soon as I heard Karl's voice on the other end, some sort of relief washed over me before I heard even more bad news, and my body shifted back into panic mode.

"I just managed to get footage from one of the paparazzi outside. Sir, it's not looking good."

I screamed at him unconsciously. "What do you mean it's not looking good? You were supposed to have eyes on both of us! What happened?"

He didn't offer me much information over the phone. Instead he just called me outside where I assumed I could see the footage.

I hurried down the marble footsteps until my eyes finally landed on Karl. My team also arrived and covered the premises fully. I approached Karl, and he moved the small screen in the camera toward me without saying a single word. My eyes landed on the video as it played. I could see Scarlet rushing toward a matte black car. As soon as she got inside the car sped toward the exit of the venue. I looked up at Karl and in my head I had already put two and two together.

The words left my mouth in an instant, "She thought it was our car?"

Karl nodded. He placed his hand on my shoulder as he

spoke. "It's alright. We're already working on tracking the car. They ditched the plate half way down eleventh Avenue but from there we're trying to get the CCTV footage from the streets and track the car."

He was still speaking but his words began to blur out in the distance. The only thing I heard was Eleventh Avenue and it all began to click in the back of my mind. I turned to Karl and shook my head. He stopped talking. The man had known me for over a decade now, and so he was able to read my expression right away.

He reached for the door of the car. "You know where she is don't you?"

I gave him a firm nod. Karl spoke up as he opened up the door of the car for me.

"I'll inform security to follow us in case things go sideways..."

I cut him off before he could go on. "I can handle this one on my own. I need you to send two of the SWAT cars to her apartment. I need to make sure her Nana is okay."

He spoke to me while he was still fixed on the road ahead. "Are you sure you don't want anyone coming with us?"

I ignored his question as I pointed toward the nearest turn and spoke, "Take a right from here and keep going straight until you see the warehouse to your left."

Karl knew questioning me further would not be worth it, so he followed my instructions instead.

My hands were carved into fists as I thought about the trouble she had gotten into because of me. I had started to feel more like a villain in her life even though all I wanted to do was to help her.

I was pushed out of my thoughts instantly when I noticed the car instantly came to a stop. I looked to my left from the window as Karl spoke up in the background. "Sir, we've arrived. Would you like me to come inside with you?"

Karl's loyalty was never questioned, but I knew exactly who I was dealing with and what I had to do. I shook my head as I spoke before I stepped out of the car.

"I've got this. I just need you to be ready. As soon as I come out with her, we need to get out of here."

He nodded, "Be safe and take care."

As I stepped out of the car, my eyes landed on the rather rundown-looking warehouse. The place had been closed for years. The street was absolutely empty. The sun had started to rise in the distance, and light began to take up the sky. Scarlet had almost been missing for hours. I prepared myself for what was about to come.

There was a rundown wooden door leading to the warehouse. It had been blocked by boxes that were piled up the front. I simply kicked the box out of the way, and the door swung open on its own. I laughed, knowing very well that they were waiting for me behind the door.

As soon as I stepped inside, the smell of fresh paint spread across the area. The huge warehouse with high ceilings was empty on the inside. The sound of my footsteps echoed around the area. I stayed still for a moment. Three doors each stood to my right and left. I waited for a few seconds before the sound of shuffling was heard from one of the beaten-down doors to my right, and I instantly hurried toward where the sound had come from.

Just when I pushed the door open, my eyes landed on three men bearing shotguns around their bodies and bullet-proof vests. I lifted both my hands upwards. It wasn't like me to surrender, but at the moment it was the only way to get Scarlet out, so I complied. All three of the men were wearing masks covering their faces. They began to surround me.

I remained still as one of them spoke into an earpiece. "He's here"

The other one turned to me and said, "Took you long enough."

I stayed silent, the man in the middle gestured toward the other two and they approached me. They began to pat me down to make sure I hadn't carried a weapon with me. Once they were done they gestured toward a door across the hallway and I began to walk toward it. My heart was thumping inside my chest. I knew exactly what, or more specifically who, I was going to find on the other side.

I stepped through the door and I was met with a dark room. A single light bulb was hanging from the ceiling. In the center of the room, there was a chair placed, and my eyes landed on her. There she was, her hair was wet, her dress was a little torn from the sides, and her wrists were zip tied to the chair. My heart sank at the sight.

I began to run toward her. I didn't even look around. Scarlet's head was tilted downwards, almost as if she had fainted.

I was halfway across the large hall where they had kept her when I heard a voice from behind me and stopped in my steps right away. "You might want to stop right there."

The voice was far too familiar. I turned around and came face to face with him. He was wearing a night blue suit perfectly catered to his body. He was a little shorter than me. His ginger-colored hair was shining under the lightbulb. I turned to face him as I spoke with anger burning up in my body.

"You've gone too far this time, Oliver."

He shrugged his shoulders as he gestured toward Scarlet. "Oh don't worry no one touched your precious. We just had a conversation until I knocked her out. Your sleeping beauty is going to be just fine, of course, as long as you comply and hand me your company's blueprints."

I knew what he wanted. I knew exactly what he was after. The moment the plan erupted in my head, I decided to take a leap of faith. "If I tell you where the plans are kept you will let us walk out of here?"

Oliver took a step closer to me. He paused for a few seconds before speaking. "I mean you know we go way back Damien and so I don't trust you."

I reached for my phone in the pocket of my trousers and showed him the screen. "This is their location. I always track them on my phone and you can even see their tracking number. Everything is there and the location is live."

He shrugged. He turned to one of his men and told them the address. As soon as the man left the room he pointed toward Scarlet. "You know I would never stoop this low but you pushed me Damien. If you just weren't so stubborn you know everything could be easier."

I stopped myself from lifting my arm and throwing a punch directly in his face. I ignored him as I ran toward Scarlet. She was still in the chair, her body was falling and slipping. I cut off both zip ties that held her hands in place and slowly lifted her head. Her eyes were closed. It seemed like she had drifted off into a deep sleep.

I turned toward Oliver. "If anything, and I mean anything happens to her I swear to God you'll be a dead man."

He remained still with his hands in his pockets as he laughed. "Oh Damien, stop it with your threats. Aren't we getting too old for all this?"

I ignored him as I carefully lifted Scarlet's body into my

arms. I carried her toward the door, and Oliver watched. All his men had their eyes following me. They were waiting for me to pull something; but, at the moment, saving Scarlet was the only thing on my mind. I ran toward the car. Karl was at the door. He pushed them open and the car was still running. As soon as I carefully placed Scarlet's body in the backseat, and ensured her head was in my lap, I gestured for Karl to go.

He pressed his foot on the pedal and we were on our way. On the way, he spoke to me. "How did you get her out without a fight?"

I sighed. "I gave them the location of my fake blueprints. And as soon as they reach the building, the FBI should be alerted. Oliver's people will trace back to him and within the coming hour hopefully, all of them will be under complete lockdown."

I noticed a smile on Karl's face.

I hoped and prayed Scarlet would be okay.

12

SCARLET

MY EYES SLOWLY BEGAN TO FLICKER OPEN. I COULD HEAR muffled sounds in the background of people talking but my vision was still blurry. Warmth was spreading through my body. My head was placed on a pillow. I tried to move but it felt as if time was moving in slow motion. I barely opened my eyes when my eyelids began to feel heavy. I could hear someone calling my name in the distance before I drifted away.

The memories slowly began returning to me. I wasn't sure if I was dreaming or if I was actually back in the room with the sociopath in the suit. I remembered his eyes had been fixed on me the entire time. The smirk on his face when I tried to shift around in my chair too much. The part that haunted me the most contained the words that fell from his mouth. He had walked so close to me that I could feel his breath upon my skin as he mocked Damien.

I gathered the courage to speak but wished I hadn't as soon as the words left my mouth. "I don't know what you have against him, but I won't give you any information about him."

I knew what he was trying to do. He was trying to scare me and turn me against Damien, but one thing he didn't know about me was that I was indeed a fighter. He took a step closer to me and narrowed his gaze as he spoke again with the same ugly smirk resting upon his face.

"You can rest assured that I'm not looking for anything from you, Sweetheart. I already have Damien right where I need him. As for you, let me enlighten you a little bit about your lover."

He clasped his hands together. I was almost afraid of what would come next, but I stayed silent as he went on. "Are you aware of his ex-wife? The woman he has a daughter with?"

As soon as I heard the words "daughter" I felt as if I was about to faint. I thought of the woman back in the bathroom. My eyes widened as I tried to make sense of everything. The man in the suit noticed the expression on my face and a smile instantly spread across his face as if he was enjoying my misery.

"Oh....dear Lord. You had no idea, did you?"

I remained silent. The last thing I wanted was to make him happier by showing just how he had taken me off guard but it was too late. My expressions had already given it all away.

He continued to speak even when I wished for him to stop. "Do you know that the mother of his child tried to fight for the custody of her daughter with all her might. Damien and I used to be friends back then. We were considering merging our companies and I remember it all vividly."

He paused, almost as if waiting for his venom-filled words to fully sink into my skin before he went on.

"Damien is a man who cares about no one but himself, and you better remember that. He threw the mother of his child into rehab and used his money, power, and influence to get full custody of his daughter. Do you really think a man capable of such a thing would ever truly love you?'

I wanted to fight for Damien and be on his side, but I couldn't forget how he had hidden the fact that he had a daughter and ex-wife from me this whole time. I wondered what else he had been hiding.

Before I could delve deeper into the nightmare of memory my body slowly began to regain consciousness. The sounds of people around me began to break through to me. My eyes slowly fluttered open. I could see streaks of sunlight falling in through the windows. A woman was speaking in the distance. Her voice was echoing in my ears.

"She is stable now..."

Before I knew it, I heard footsteps on the wooden floors below. A familiar voice rang in my ears. I turned my head toward the left and there she was. Nana looked worried. Her eyes looked tired- almost as if she hadn't slept at all.

She instantly grabbed onto my hand. "Never do that to me again. Do you know how worried I was for you? I thought I almost lost you."

A smile spread across my face as soon as I looked at her. It felt as if all my worries melted away. I moved my body forward and instantly wrapped my arms around her. She was holding on to me for dear life as if I would disappear from her arms at any moment.

I sighed while she squeezed my body closer to hers. "Nana, I'm okay. I promise he didn't touch a single hair on my head."

Before I could go on Nana cut me off, "Yeah, I would have personally cut his arms off if he tried my love."

I let out a small laugh. I was about to tell her not to worry about me too much but a small knock on the door cut me off. My eyes landed on the door and there seemed to be a doctor in the doorway. She wore her white coat and her hair was tied up in a ponytail. She smiled at the two of us before she spoke.

"If it's okay may I have a few moments with the patient."

I could see from Nana's expression that she was ready to fight the poor woman in the doorway as soon as she was told to leave me alone. I gently placed my hand over Nana's shoulder and told her I would be okay. After some hesitation, she told me she would be just outside the door if I needed her.

As soon as the door closed, and I was alone with the doctor, I squeezed my eyes shut. "What is it doctor? Please tell me it's not too bad?"

I was mentally preparing for some sort of an injury or illness to be disclosed; however, the woman placed her hand over mine gently. She made sure to keep eye contact with me as she spoke in a low tone. "Scarlet, firstly I'd like to tell you that you haven't suffered any injuries or illness from this whole situation."

I let out a breath of fresh air however she was not done yet. Her eyes drifted away from me as she continued to speak. "I would like to inform you though Scarlet, while my team was conducting our check-up and making sure you were fully okay, we discovered that you're pregnant."

At first, I thought I had heard her wrong. Maybe I was still dreaming. I began to pinch my arms slowly and she noticed what I was doing. She placed her hand back gently over mine as she spoke.

"You're not dreaming Scarlet. This is real and you are around three weeks into the pregnancy. I suggest you have a conversation with the father and decide whether you want to keep the child or not."

I nodded my head. I still couldn't believe what she had said. A part of me was still numb to the news. Damien was the only person I had slept with in the past three weeks. In my head, it was dating down to the first time we hooked up, and it all started to make sense to me. I was about to ask her more about the pregnancy, but both of us paused for a mere moment when we heard a knock on the door. My heart was still sinking. I couldn't breathe properly when my eyes landed on Damien from the corner of the room. He was standing behind the door staring at me. I could tell he wanted to come inside. A part of me was angry at him, but the other part of me was still startled at the fact that I was carrying his child.

I decided to swallow my anger and first see what he said.

I looked over at the doctor and thanked her for the information. She offered me a good recovery and then headed out of the door.

This was the part that gave me the most anxiety-being left alone with Damien. I had no idea what to say. I had too much potential information about him and I didn't even know where to begin. I decided to keep quiet and let him do all the talking. A part of me wanted to confront him straight away but I decided to take things slow.

Damien took a few slow steps into the room. He refused to look me in the eyes. I felt as if something was off. Damien's head was held down, his shoulders were slouched. Before sitting on the bed close to me, he pointed toward the empty space next to me and spoke in a low tone. "May I sit?"

I offered him a nod but I refused to speak. My heart skipped a beat as he sat down close to me. He finally looked up at me and that was when I noticed that his eyes looked red almost as if he had been crying. Tears began to form in his eyes. He took my hand gently almost as if he was afraid of hurting me. My heart was aching for him. I wanted to grab him and just wrap my arms around his body but I stayed still as he spoke.

"I have no words to express how sorry I am for all this. Scarlet, I love you from the bottom of my heart. I do. But I fear all I'm doing is bringing danger into your life and causing you pain. It's better if we keep our distance. As dear as you are to me I cannot fathom losing you at my expense."

He paused. His voice cracked. My heart was breaking. He had said he loved me for the first time but the words that followed made me feel like he had just ended things with me. I was about to say something but stopped when Damien spoke up again. "My assistant has emailed your full-time contract at Corelli Enterprise to you already. It's a very comfortable position, and you will be taken care of by all my people."

I couldn't help it. The words just fell out of my mouth. Even though I had a lot to lose and too many fears in the back of my mind, like the fact that I was pregnant and everything I was sacrificing-my safety and Nana's safety among many other things, I wondered deep down if loving Damien and fighting for him was even worth it? But I needed to know what he was thinking.

"What about us?"

He let go of my hand immediately, and I felt the distance between us. Damien stood up. I could sense that the conversation was not going anywhere. I knew he was feeling too much in the moment and I had to wait before I dropped the big news on him so I decided to remain calm even though every part of my body wanted to ask him all the questions in my head.

As he stood up he brought his body closer to me. He spoke, "For now you really need this job, Scarlet, and I really need you to be safe. My number one priority is to keep you safe. I cannot keep hurting you, and I cannot be why you end up in a scandal with your boss."

I sighed. I didn't understand why this was happening. Why we couldn't be together? The question fell from my mouth without much consideration. "Damien, why can't we just be together. None of this is making sense to me."

He paused. "I promise to keep my eye on you, to keep you safe, but for now from a distance. Scarlet right now you need this job. While you work for me we cannot be in a relationship. Being in a relationship with an employee, a subordinate, will not only damage my position as CEO, it will damage my reputation as a former marine officer. I need to put you first and I need to save the both of us from the hell these news outlets and magazines will put us through professionally. I have deep responsibilities as a businessman and someone who took an oath for this country.

He didn't really give me a chance to say anything at all. He moved forward and placed a kiss upon my forehead. He refused to allow his eyes to fall on me. My heart skipped a beat as he turned his back toward me and began walking out the door.

Just as he reached the door he turned to me. He had forced a smile on his face as he spoke one last time.

"I'm sorry Scarlet; but, I promise everything will make sense with time."

I nodded before he spoke again, "You better turn up to work on time on Monday. This is your boss speaking."

I watched as he had completely turned into someone detached from their emotions.

I wanted a hug but he did not. I felt as if he was being too cold toward me and my heart skipped a beat in fear. "Damien, why are you being this way?"

He turned to me, and for a moment I couldn't even recognize him as he spoke. "I'm doing this for the both of us. It needs to be done and the sooner you wake up the better. The real world doesn't allow us to be together. As I said before, focus on your work and I'll focus on mine. Don't end up ruining this opportunity I'm giving you."

It felt as if he was referring to me like he owned me. I wondered if this was the type of man I wanted my heart to get attached to in the end-the type of person who would choose his reputation and work before me.

Was this really what I wanted?

How could he treat me like I was nothing in the blink of an eye?

13

SCARLET

MONDAY HAD SWUNG AROUND FASTER THAN I HAD EVER wanted it to. This whole time had been spent with Damien's guards circling my apartment and the hospital at all times. I had been in recovery for about five days and hadn't spoken to Damien at all. Nana had been on edge the entire time and told me to turn down the job Damien had offered with every chance she got. Deep down she knew I was never going to do that. We both saw the bills and the rent piling up once again, and if I ever wanted to make it as a writer I had to start with a stable job.

Before I knew it my recovery period was over. The nights had been spent in a rather lonely manner. Every part of me wanted to text Damien and check on him, maybe ask if he could talk, but there was a lot holding me back. The words the man had said to me when I had been taken kept spinning around in the back of my mind. I didn't know if I could really trust the man whose child I was carrying; but, at the same time, he was the only person who had done everything in their power for me. I knew deep down things with

Damien were not over. He was just on edge after he almost lost me.

As the car Damien had sent for me stopped before the Corelli headquarters, I thanked Karl and stepped out toward the entrance. There was no trace of the shooting that occurred there only a few weeks ago.

I had a plan in the back of my mind and was going to stick to it. I wouldn't let the drama of my personal life with Damien get in the middle of my job. I kept on a straight face as I walked into the large building and just as I made my way to the reception desk my eyes landed on a familiar face.

The sound of Tory's heels was once again clicking all over the place. As soon as I walked into the building I felt the stares of the rest of the employees burning holes into my body. I tried to ignore them all. Tory's eyes landed on me from behind the reception desk and she instantly put down the tablet in her hands. She didn't even care about the people staring. The woman came toward me and instantly wrapped me in her arms pulling me into a firm hug.

She whispered into my ear in a polite and low tone. "How are you holding up my love?"

I tried to keep on a straight face as she pulled away. She began to walk toward the elevator and I followed right behind her as I replied to her in a steady tone. "I'm doing alright. I just want to focus on my job and get it right. I read through the manuals you sent me and I already practiced how to schedule appointments and everything."

As the elevator doors closed behind me, Tory turned to face me. Her expression shifted as she spoke.

"I wasn't asking about how capable you are to handle being Damien's secretary, Scarlet. I know you've got it. I was asking about how you are holding up with what Damien pulled."

She seemed annoyed at just mentioning his name. I sighed. I didn't know if I was ready to talk about it; but, I felt like I trusted Tory. "To be honest I can see where he is coming from. I mean did you see the stares I was getting from the people here just because of the magazines and the news after the ball."

She nodded. "I know, but, there are other ways to deal with these situations. Damien is pulling a classic him. He's just trying to run from what makes him vulnerable. In this case, we're talking about a who."

Her eyes rolled back to me and I couldn't help but blush momentarily.

As we walked out of the elevator I couldn't help it. The question just came straight out of my mouth. "Do you think he would be willing to see me?"

Tory turned around. A smirk was spread on her face as she gave me a little wink. "Of course he would. He gets free from all of his meetings in about an hour or so."

I nodded as I followed Tory into what looked to be one of the fanciest halls I had ever seen. A large chandelier was hanging from the ceiling with diamonds glistening on it, marble-coated floors were shining below my heels, and the entire area had been designed in a modern manner with whites and blacks blending together ever so perfectly.

I was still in awe by the area I was standing in when Tory gestured toward a large reception desk in the far right corner of the hallway. It was an oval-shaped desk with LED lights built around the edges, and a rather fancy-looking desk chair was placed behind the reception desk. I was still staring at the area around me when Tory spoke up.

"This is where you will be working. You have a computer there with all the appointments you need to book for the day. And I had a shared notes space where I will add anything else if needed."

I nodded while I tried to contain my excitement. Just as Tory was about to bid me goodbye I called out for her and she turned around instantly. "Uh Tory, one last question. Where does Damien work?"

I knew I needed to have a conversation with him by the end of the day. There was too much between us that was still not decided and I hadn't forgotten that I was still carrying his child. I waited until a smile appeared on Tory's face as she spoke. "Turn around Scarlet. You're in for a surprise."

As soon as I turned around my eyes widened. There was a wooden door leading toward what looked to be an office; but, I couldn't see much as the door was closed. Next to the door was a nameplate,

"Damien Corelli: CEO."

My heart skipped a beat. My jaw dropped for a mere moment. I turned back to face Tory and she was just enjoying the look on my face. She threw her hands up in the air in defense as she spoke just before she walked back toward the elevator leaving me behind. "He likes to keep the special ones close to him-you know an arm's length and all."

Her words rang in the back of my mind. The entire hour that came after my interaction with Tory was spent filled with anxiety by me. I couldn't even sit still for too long, and every time the phone on my desk rang I would jump up to answer the client. My job was going pretty well, I couldn't really say the same for my mental health. I felt like I would have a heart attack the moment Damien walked through the doors. He had broken up with me a few days ago and he had placed me right in front of his office at the same time. I didn't understand what game he was playing.

Around two hours had passed, and I had just put down

the phone after setting up an appointment and directing another client toward one of the board members when I finally felt I could breathe fresh air. I had barely even moved from my seat when I heard the bell of the elevator reaching my floor. My heart sank for a mere moment. My head turned toward the elevator down the hall and before I knew it the double doors opened up to a very familiar face.

He was dressed head to toe in a perfectly fitted and styled suit. His hair was styled in place with each strand of jet black refusing to fall toward his forehead. There were two women following behind him with tablets in their hands and Bluetooth devices in their ears. As soon as Damien stepped out of the elevator, his eyes darted toward the reception desk, toward me to be specific.

I couldn't help it. I instantly moved my gaze away from him as my whole body felt shivers running through me. He walked toward his office right behind my desk and just as I thought the awkward passing would be over he decided to stop right by my desk. Damien carefully leaned on the desk as he placed his elbow on the marble surface. His eyes were fixed on my face but I refused to look up at him. "Ms. Hayes, how is your first day going so far?"

The women with the tablets were still there. His eyes were still fixed on me. My anxiety was through the roof as I cleared my throat and spoke in a low tone.

"It's going great."

He nodded. I knew deep down he wanted nothing more than for me to lift my head and look him in the eyes but I wasn't going to give him that.

After he headed inside, I waited for what felt like forever but it was actually only thirty minutes. That's when both of the women walked out of his office and down the hallway. I knew he was alone inside, and as much as I wanted to stay quiet there was a storm going on my mind that he had caused and I wanted answers for everything.

I pushed myself to turn toward the double doors leading to his office. I raised my fist and knocked on the door and instantly I heard him.

"COME IN."

He paused before he merely looked up at me and continued to say,

"Lock the door please."

14

SCARLET

HE LOOKED OVER AT ME WITH SURPRISE WRITTEN ALL OVER HIS face. He gestured for me to close and lock the door so I did. The office was the size of my dream home. His desk had been placed in front of wall-sized windows, and a huge cabinet of alcohol was placed in the corner along with an expensive rug and a sofa set. As soon as I closed the door behind me, he raised an eyebrow as he spoke.

"Are you having trouble with updating my schedule Ms. Hayes? Would you like for me to call Tory?'

I rolled my eyes. His attitude had started to make me feel angry, and before I knew it, I had stomped my way to the front of his desk. I made sure to bend down slowly until there was merely an inch between the two of us as I spoke with anger burning up in my body.

"So you're just going to treat me like I'm some employee now?! Is that really how it's going to be between us from now on Damien?"

He looked up at me and I watched the spark of anger rising in his body. His emerald green eyes were glistening back at me. I felt the anger inside of me melting but I had to hold my ground. We had been through too much for me to just be treated like an employee. The way he was treating me was making me feel like he never loved me at all. I wondered if fighting for him and wanting to stay with him was even the best choice to make in the moment.

I waited with my chest heaving up and down with anger as he finally cleared his throat and spoke rather loudly. "What do you want me to do Scarlet? Do you understand that you almost died? Your life was in danger because of me?"

The anger rose in his voice.

"I'm tired of telling you the same shit again and again! I swear Scarlet sometimes you just act dumb. I'm treating you like an employee because that's who you are. I cannot be out there treating you like some princess in front of the people of my company. Do you not understand? I'm the CEO here. It's not a joke. You're not in a fairytale. Please grow up!"

It seemed as if the part of him fueled by anger was coming back and I stepped back for a moment. Damien stayed in his seat. I watched as he threw the black colored pen he had in his hand across the desk.

I was actually scared of him for a moment. The same doubts ran across my mind once again. Did he really even love me? Was all of this worth fighting for? Is this who I wanted to father my child?

He wasn't done yet. The anger was still not completely out. I could see that his hands were curved into fists as he yelled, "You're not the only one whose future is at stake here Scarlet. Open your eyes for once!"

I knew he was trying to take everything he was feeling out on me, but I ignored him and his outburst of anger as I rolled my eyes at him with annoyance filling up my body. "You asked me what I want right?" I took a pause before I went on. "Damien you broke up with me. You left me for your reputation and your company. How do you think it makes me feel? I was willing to fight for you but now I don't even know if I want to be with someone who will choose his company over me?"

I watched as the anger in his eyes began to calm down but not fully yet. He placed his fingers between his eyebrows as if he was stressed and he yelled at me again.

"Scarlet, I told you the first day I met you. Falling into an entanglement with me never ends well. Women have always ended up running scared from the chaos of my life. But you know what has stayed? My work and the company that I built from the ground up. It has never disappointed me and I would give my life for it."

He paused, and my heart broke for a moment. I wondered if he ever loved me at all; but, what he said next pushed some of my doubts away.

"Just like I would give my life to protect you, I don't want you to think I don't love you. I do but in matters like these I'm not just choosing myself I'm also choosing to keep you safe."

I sighed. I decided I wouldn't leave without the answers I wanted. "For once I want you to be honest with me. I want you to tell me if you have a daughter who is I don't even know how old, I want you to tell me why you sent her mother to rehab, and that you have a whole ex-wife! Yes, I was kidnapped but it wasn't all because of you. I chose to be in your life, Damien. I chose to go to that party and I chose to leave. I am not asking you for much but if I'm still choosing to be a part of your life can you please just protect me by not running and hiding very important information from me?"

As soon as the words left my mouth, I saw a sudden

change in his reaction toward me. He jolted upwards suddenly, and before I knew it, he was just inches away from me. His eyes were wide as the words left his mouth. I could feel his breath brushing against my skin, and I almost flinched for a moment when I thought that he was going to get mad at me. But what happened next took me by surprise.

He moved forward and instantly wrapped his arms around me. He pulled me close to his body.

As he was holding me close, he whispered, "I'm sorry, I never meant to make you feel like I'm pushing you away or running or hiding information from you. I just got so scared. I couldn't imagine losing you."

I nodded as he took my hand and began walking toward the couch set on the other side of the office. I sat down next to him and it seemed as if he just couldn't keep his hands away from me. He held my hands in his as he turned to face me. I was taken by another surprise when Damien, of all people, the CEO of one of the largest companies in the country, knelt down on the ground in front of me. My heart skipped a beat as he pulled out his phone and after a few swipes, he turned the screen toward me.

My eyes landed on the screen and I could see a picture of a girl who looked to be around eleven years old. She had dark jet-black hair and Damien's eyes. She was smiling at the camera, and holding what seemed to be a piece of candy.

He pointed at the screen while still kneeling down on the floor in front of me. "Scarlet, this is my daughter Isabella. She just turned twelve and she is the light of my life. She lives in New York with my Mom because she did not want to move here and switch schools, have to make new friends, etc. I had her at a very tough time in my life but she has changed the way I view the world completely."

I stared at him as he paused for a moment, I could see that the topic was very sensitive for him and he was having trouble going on and so I ran my thumb over his hand as I made sure to speak in a calm tone.

"She's beautiful Damien and she has your eyes."

A small laugh escaped his lips. "She has my anger too. You should see her when her needs aren't met."

Both of us laughed at the little joke before I noticed his eyes turned back to being serious. He cleared his throat as he kept his gaze on me before continuing to speak. "Scarlet the reason I never mentioned her to you was because my daughter is a completely different world to me. I think it's no secret that we have a huge age difference. I feared you would run from me if you found out I already had a child. And the story with her mother is just as complicated. I just wanted to make sure you would be ready before I dropped a bomb on you."

I nodded before speaking, "Damien, why would I mind you having a daughter? I've almost died by just knowing you. Also, have you seen me around kids? I love them. If she means the world to you, I want to meet her."

He smiled at me almost in a bittersweet manner. "I'm just glad you didn't react the way I thought you would. You most definitely will meet her and I have a feeling she is going to love you."

I pulled my hands forward, almost begging him to get off the floor and sit next to me but he shook his head signaling that he wasn't done yet.

He took a deep breath before he went on. "When I met her mother I fell in love and that is no lie. I thought I had met the love of my life but she was an actress. And when she began to get bigger roles Scarlet the industry just sucked her in. She was an amazing person when I met her but you know how it is behind the scenes in Hollywood."

I nodded along making sure to stay attentive to his story.

"A year after Isabella was born her mother fell into hard drugs with the producers and actors in her movies. She would be at these launches and she would drink too much, take pills, and do a lot more. For a year I tried and I tried to make it work. I tried to get her the best help but nothing worked until the day she left Bella with one of the maids and the woman tried to kidnap my daughter for money."

I felt my heart skipping a beat, He had tears in his eyes. He couldn't even speak as he took a deep breath trying to hold his tears. I moved forward, wrapped my arms around his body, pulled him closer to me. I couldn't bear to watch the way he was breaking in front of me.

I whispered to him slowly in the calmest way possible when I could feel his body shivering close to me.

"It's okay Damien. It's alright if you aren't ready to talk about it with me yet. I can wait until you are ready."

He shook his head, pulled himself away from me, and I could see that he was fighting back tears as he spoke. "I just want you to know that I didn't just send the mother of my child to a rehab to get rid of her. I tried everything in my power until it got out of hand and she had to go for her to get better."

I nodded. Everything I had heard and all the anger inside of me just melted. I instantly wrapped my arms around him before I pulled him closer to me and before he even knew what hit him our lips crashed into each others. I closed my eyes and placed both my hands on either side of his face as I kept him as close to me as possible.

In the moment the world around me began to spin out of motion. Everything was happening so fast. He grasped the front of my top and before I knew it he had lifted me upwards. My back fell onto the surface of the couch in his office. I looked up and Damien's shirt was already halfway off of his body. As he came down close to me I gripped onto his back and tilted my head upwards, my nails dug further into his back when he bit down on my neck causing a moan to escape my lips.

His hand moved down to the middle of my skirt and as soon as his fingers made contact with my clit another moan escaped my lips. He dug two of his fingers deep inside of me and whispered into my ear as his other palm went over my mouth covering my lips.

"You're going to have to keep it down in here princess."

I felt my soul leaving my body as he bit down harder on my neck and he pressed his hands tighter onto my mouth stopping me from moaning any further. His fingers were deep inside me moving in and out, and I could hear how wet I was just for him.

Damien pulled away for a moment and began to unbutton my shirt. My skirt had been pulled up and he had spread my legs on the couch. The sun was setting in the distance and I could feel like every single part of my body was tingling for him. I wanted him more and more by the second.

His hands had cupped my breasts, his lips were all over me, he was making sure to kiss every inch of my body before I carefully reached up and tugged at the belt holding his trousers in place. He stared back at me with a smirk spread across his face.

He pulled me closer to him by grabbing me by the back of my head as he spoke into my ear.

"You promise you're going to be a good girl and not make any noise?"

I stared back at him by narrowing my gaze and making sure to blink twice before I nodded my head almost instantly. He pushed me backward onto the couch and began to unbuckle his belt. He spread my legs and pulled them upwards until they were resting on his shoulders. I grabbed his back even tighter as he pushed himself inside of me. I squeezed my eyes shut and suddenly the pain mixed with pleasure spread through my body. I was taking deep breaths as he thrust in and out of me, his pace got faster and faster by the moment. Just as he was about to come, he pulled out of me. The white liquid landed on my stomach and I breathed out.

Damien breathed out heavily. He pulled himself away from me and then moved forward. He gently kissed my forehead.

I smiled as he whispered to me. "You really were a good girl weren't you? Let me clean you up."

He ran toward the desk, grabbed a stack of tissues and wet wipes, walked over to me, and began to clean my stomach. I was looking up at him and smiling. He had noticed the way I was endearingly staring at him, his shirt was still off, and I could see his abs were perfectly toned. He had a well taken care of body.

He smiled up at me as he spoke,

"What's up? Anything on your mind?"

I shook my head. "Nothing, I'm just thinking my first day at work is not going as planned is it?"

He laughed as he shrugged his shoulders and spoke. "Yeah we really need to be more careful about things like this from now on. I don't want the tabloids catching something from a hidden camera in the sky or some bullshit."

I knew what he meant. A comfortable sense of silence began to spread between the two of us. I felt as if the timing was right. He had opened up to me more than I could ever imagine. At the moment he stirred two cups of coffee for the two of us and sat down on the couch wrapped in his work jacket. We were staring out into the endless sky with the sun on its way to fully setting when the words just fell from my mouth without even considering what would come next.

"Damien, I'm pregnant."

15

DAMIEN

As soon as the words left her mouth I felt as if my heart stopped in my chest. The mugs of coffee were still placed in front of me. My hands shook, but when I looked up and saw the look on Scarlet's face I knew I couldn't show her the fact that I was just as anxious and scared as her. I could not for a moment believe what she had just said.

I could see that she was waiting for me to react and she seemed nervous as she stared at me. In my experience with life so far I have learned not to react right away when someone is expecting something from me. I tried to stay calm as I waited for the coffee to be done. Scarlet was staring at me from the couch. Her gaze didn't dare to move from me.

I finished carrying the two cups of coffee and carefully placed them on the coffee table in front of us. As I turned to face her, a small smile spread across her face.

She raised her eyebrows. "Did you hear me? Damien, I'm pregnant?"

I kept a smile on my face even though I was just as nervous as her on the inside. I wondered about what this would mean for the two of us, would this end up making or breaking us? I moved forward and gently took her hand into my own as I spoke. "Scarlet, if you expect for me to react in a bad way I'm sorry but you can take my reaction as the happiest man alive right now."

I knew deep down that everything would be dealt with slowly. She was merely a kid to me. I had lived through life enough to know not to show an overreaction at the moment. Instead, my job was to calm her down. I moved forward and wrapped my arms around her immediately pulling her into a tight hug. I felt as if a weight had been lifted off of my shoulders. I took a deep breath as she moved closer and held on to me.

Once her breathing had settled down, she spoke. "So you want to keep it, the child? I need to know what is going on in your head, Damien, because I'm so afraid right now."

She hadn't said another word when I pulled away from her. Her gaze was resting upon me as I spoke. "Scarlet I'm in my forties. I have more fortune than I can ever use in my lifetime and I don't care about money or business anymore. The only thing that is important to me now is my family. The people I love and hold dear to me. You telling me that I have the opportunity to bring a child into the world with you, the woman who has completely and utterly stolen my heart is the best news I could ever receive."

I wasn't even done speaking yet when I noticed that tears were forming around the corners of her eyes. I paused for a moment before I went on. "Listen, at the end of the day the decision is yours to make and I will support you in every way. But I'm just telling you if you decide to keep this child I promise to give you both the most comfortable and bright life in my power."

Scarlet sighed, and pulled away from me for a moment.

"I know that right now you're being all optimistic, Damien, but I saw the way you broke up with me, treated me like an employee, and now you want to bring a child into this world, your world to be specific. Are you forgetting just how dangerous your world is?"

I could see that everything was getting to her. I narrowed my gaze at her. I knew she was waiting for me to say something until I finally gathered the courage to speak.

"Scarlet, I know my world is full of dangers but I can promise you I won't let the chaos of my life get to my kids. They will always be fully protected until the end and that is a promise of mine. You know I'm not one to take promises lightly."

Scarlet looked over at me, and I could see the anxiety in her eyes when she spoke. "It's not that I doubt the fact that you won't be able to give the child a comfortable life but Damien let's not forget you are living in chaos. I might adjust to it but is your world really safe to bring a child into? Apart from that there is a lot I haven't done yet. I want to be an established writer and my career when it comes to writing is just on the back burner. Having a child is a huge responsibility. What if I decide to have a child and it ends up meaning I will have to give up my passion and my career at such a young age?"

I moved closer to her and wrapped my arms around her. We were cuddling on the couch in my office as I spoke to her in the calmest tone possible. "I understand the fears and the doubts going through your head. I know that things are all happening at once and I know that you are overwhelmed."

I could see her eyes as they were fixed on me. She was nodding along as I spoke, and I made sure to keep my gaze rested on her.

"I'm clearing our schedules starting tomorrow and

throughout the Christmas holidays. One of the secretaries will handle your work and you're coming with me on a 'business' trip. Business is a lot slower this time of the year anyway."

She stared at me with a look of utter surprise written all across her face. She had no idea what I had in mind. "We're going on a surprise trip planned by yours truly, and if by the end of it, if you want I can take you to see the best doctor in the country and she can give you all the options you have regarding this big decision and how much time you have to make it."

I knew just as soon as the words had left my mouth she calmed down a bit. I instantly pulled her body closer to mine when it felt like everything was going to be okay. I placed a kiss on her lips as I spoke once again. "How does that sound?"

She smiled, and my shoulder was finally slouched and the anxiety had left my body when I heard her reply.

"It sounds like a plan I guess."

"And since I am sharing everything, keep this in mind. We still need to be vigilant because the fight isn't over. Oliver, the one responsible for all the attacks, is bribing his way out of the FBI as we speak. I know there will be revenge very soon. But as I said earlier, Scarlet, I promise to keep us safe.

The anxiety that left the room for a fleeting moment, returned.

16

DAMIEN

The Christmas holidays had started. I had just ended a long phone call with Scarlet's grandmother and the woman had been hard to convince. My plan had been laid out in front of her but it was safe to say she had some trust issues ever since the shooting. I knew I had been tough with Scarlet. My anger had gotten the best of me at times and I had hurt her. Taking her on a trip to New York was part of my plan to improve things for us.

I had made sure my security was circling me and Scarlet as well as her grandma too. I needed to be sure everyone was safe until all my enemies were put behind bars for good.

I had a long conversation with Tory. She warned me again that if the public saw me with Scarlet and she did not have an engagement ring on her finger my reputation would be in shambles and my position as CEO would be compromised. I planned on putting the anxiety of us not being able to be together openly to an end as well. A Christmas holiday trip to New York would solve many problems between us and hopefully convince Scarlet to keep the child she was now carrying.

I was pulled out of my thoughts when my eyes drifted toward the window and there she was on the way up. I had made sure for Karl to pick Scarlet up in secret so the tabloids and the dangerous enemies of mine would be unaware.

She looked as stunning as ever, wearing a black knitted sweater with a skirt and some leggings. My eyes glazed over her and a smile appeared across my face when I saw a backpack on her shoulders. I had specifically told her to pack only an overnight bag with everything she thought she needed. Secretly my plan was for us to be staying at my family home in New York. If she needed more clothes or anything for that matter, I would buy them while there. I wanted to keep her as calm and stress-free as possible. Scarlet's Nana had gone over to her sister's place for the holidays, and I had made sure my security was protecting them so the worry of leaving her behind was gone from the back of both of our minds. I had also gotten her blessing with a little bit of my charm for the holiday trip to New York.

As soon as the elevator doors opened up, and she walked through the doors, her eyes widened. I was watching her from afar and I knew she was reacting to the surprise I had for her. For a mere moment, she just remained standing there as her eyes gazed over the roof of the building and I knew it wasn't what she had expected it to be. It was a huge open area with a bar to the left, and in the middle of the open space was a landing pad. I had made sure for us to get to New York fashionably. On the landing pad was a small private jet. Its engine was running in the middle of the roof. I stood next to the pilot waiting for her to walk up to me.

When I noticed that she wasn't moving any time soon and she was too overwhelmed with it all, I ran toward her. As I approached her, I opened my arms, from habit and she fell into them. I wrapped my arms around her and she grabbed onto me tightly as I heard her speaking in a muffled tone while her face was buried in my suit jacket. "Damien, what's going on? What is all of this?"

I turned toward the pilot and then back at her before I spoke equally as loud for both to hear me due to the loud sound of the jet's engine running in the background. "Remember I am a man that keeps promises so I'm taking you to New York for the Christmas Holidays. I think it's about time you meet my family."

I saw the instant look of surprise painted across her face. She pulled away from me and she was about to speak but I was already prepared for what she had to say. So I carefully placed my fingers gently on her lips shutting her up as I spoke. "Don't worry about Nana. I talked to her already. She gave me her blessing. And if you need more clothes, toiletries, or whatever I will buy it there."

I knew she had no other argument to tell me why she couldn't go. She looked over at me and narrowed her gaze. "So you want me to meet your family now? I thought I was just an employee to you?"

I knew she was teasing me because I had said this to her in one of my fits of anger.

I couldn't help but smile. I stared back at her and brushed off the words she had said to me as I offered her my hand. "You ready to go?"

She nodded firmly and I didn't wait for a second longer as I pulled her toward the jet. We sat in the back, and I grabbed Scarlet's hand as tightly as I possibly could. I noticed she had never done anything like this before. I wanted to let her know she was safe with me.

As the plane took off, I noticed the way she grabbed onto me tighter. Her nerves were growing.

"Just leave all the worry behind and enjoy the view," I said.

I took a deep breath and when I noticed we had left the building behind, my eyes focused on the window outside, and I could see the beauty of nature below.

I pointed toward the window on Scarlet's side and drew her attention toward the view beneath us. For a mere second, Scarlet tilted her head to face me, and something came over me at the moment and I pushed my body toward her. I had instantly taken her by surprise when my lips crashed against hers. Scarlet did the one thing that she knew would turn me on the most. She simply and rather innocently bit my bottom lip causing me to pull her that much closer to me. She was a pro at teasing me and turning me on.

As I grabbed her by the back of her hair, I whispered in her ear with dominance taking over my body. "You really should not have done that princess."

She gulped as I reached for her neck and bit down on her collar bone. A moan escaped her mouth right away. I placed my hand upon her thigh, and at the same time, I kept her mouth occupied by my lips. I wasn't giving her room to breathe as I pressed my lips further onto hers.

A gasp escaped her mouth when my hand brushed under her skirt. My fingers were now placed on her clit and she was quivering underneath me. A smile spread across my face as I decided to give her a little bit of a hard time.

I made sure to look her dead in the eyes as I spoke to her with my fingers now fully inside of her as her body was shaking underneath me.

"You really thought you would tease me and get away with it?"

Scarlet's eyes were wide with pleasure. Her head was

lying back against the seat with her whole body fully in my control. I placed another kiss on her lips before I lifted her body with one hand and flipped her around. She gasped and as soon as she was face down on the jet's leather seat I carefully lifted her skirt from the back. The thong she wore under her skirt had already gotten wet.

A smile spread across my lips as I gently ran my fingers over her ass. I could feel the goosebumps rising over her body as I spoke. "You might have to think twice before teasing me next time princess."

Before she knew what was coming, I lifted my left hand and within a second, it collided to her ass cheeks causing a loud slapping sound to fill the jet. I pulled her upwards with her hair and as soon as her face was closer to mine, I made sure to grab onto her tightly. "So, what did we learn today?"

She was breathless; her face turned red and her lipstick was smudged. I brought my hand over to her throat making it harder for her to speak. "Don't tease you without asking."

I nodded as I let her go. I placed a small kiss on her forehead and her body instantly curled up closer to mine.

As the ride continued and Scarlet was focused on the view outside my thoughts began to wander.

Was I really making the right move?

I knew deep down I loved her but I wondered if putting my reputation and my company in danger for a woman was the right thing to do. I wondered if it would all be worth it in the end. Seeing her happy was important to me, but what if her happiness came at the cost of my company? Many fears were running through my mind.

I had barely even noticed when the plane touched the ground at once. I turned to Scarlet and told her that we were now getting off. She held on to me and as soon as we landed Scarlet was about to say something as she reached for the door to her right thinking that she was going to step out when I grabbed her gently by the side of her face. I knew that I had taken her by surprise and she barely had a moment to even see it coming. I went straight for it, my lips crashed into her's and I felt at home. Scarlet grabbed me and what was just a mere set of seconds felt like a lifetime with her.

As I pulled away from her the door to my left opened up. We both stepped out of the jet that was still running. I looked around and finally felt like I was in my comfort zone. New York was my home and I couldn't wait for Scarlet to see it. We were on top of one of the highest buildings in the city. Before we had even landed the rooftop was already surrounded by security. I could see the lights below me almost like stars in the sky. My heart skipped a beat when I turned toward the door of the rooftop. I could imagine her running toward me. My Bella.

I heard her voice in the distance. My body flipped around immediately and I came face-to-face with the door. It swung open from the distance and there she was. Isabella came running toward me at full speed. I did the same. Her shiny black hair was blowing with the wind as she instantly wrapped her arms around my body providing me with warmth. The little girl held onto me and I knew it deep in my heart that she had missed me more than life itself.

She spoke up as soon as she was in my arms. "I missed you so much, Daddy. You said you would come earlier this Christmas!"

I laughed as I placed a gentle kiss on her left cheek. I immediately spoke up in her ear as she was in my arms. "I promise I'll make it up to you on Christmas Day. I didn't mean to be late, daddy was just a little too caught up with work. I'm here now and I'm not going anywhere for a while."

Before she could answer I began twirling her around in my arms and she started to laugh out loud. From the corner of my eye, I could see Scarlet had an endearing smile spread across her face as she saw the two of us.

I placed Bella down on the ground carefully and Scarlet walked closer to the two of us.

Bella's laugh spread across the entire rooftop and I couldn't help but smile. She was dancing around with happiness. She hadn't even noticed Scarlet yet, I wondered how she would react to meeting someone new. Scarlet was the first woman I had ever introduced to my daughter and I wondered if she would like her.

I was willing to take the risk. I wanted my daughter to meet the woman who had stolen my heart and made me do things I would never have considered. I drew a deep breath in before I knelt down and spoke. While I was speaking, Bella wrapped her arms around my shoulders and listened to me attentively. "Belle, this is Scarlet, Scarlet, Bella."

I pointed between the two of them and anxiety rushed to my body. Scarlet instantly knelt down and I watched the way she extended her hand forward for Bella to shake. Scarlet had a sweet smile on her face and she looked genuinely happy to see my daughter.

Bella moved a loose strand of black hair away from her eyes and tucked it neatly behind her ear as she watched Scarlet. Scarlet spoke up in the most gentle tone. "Hi honey. It's nice to meet you."

She had just extended her hand forward but to my surprise, Bella pulled Scarlet in for a tight hug. My eyes widened at this. I hadn't imagined for her to be this open so soon. Watching them hug gave me a sense of peace like a weight had been lifted off my shoulders.

I decided to lighten the moment up with a little joke.

Bella loved when I kindly bullied her and she would always laugh at my sarcasm.

"Easy there Bella don't end up crushing her bones."

I noticed that before Bella let Scarlet go she whispered in her ear but her words were directed toward me.

"But she smells so nice, and she's so pretty. Daddy have you seen her hair? It's so beautiful. It looks just like mommy's hair used to!"

I turned to face Scarlet. I was shocked for a moment. I didn't know what to say at the connection my daughter had made. It was probably the reason I had warmed up to Scarlet so soon too. I noticed the way her eyes were glimmering with just pure happiness. I pulled Bella toward me and nodded my head at her. Scarlet knelt closer to Bella and pointed at her hair as she spoke. "Oh please! I'm so jealous of your haircut and your eyes. They're the brightest I have ever seen."

Bella smiled instantly. It was as if Scarlet had made her day with just a few compliments. She spoke up and this time her tone was more high-pitched and full of energy. "Daddy, I like her. Is she going to stay with us?"

My heart couldn't help but burst with a sense of calmness. I turned to face Scarlet as I slowly stood up and pulled Bella. We began to walk toward the main door leading down to the building we had landed in. I turned to Scarlet. "I mean that's the plan but you have to keep being sweet to her and maybe she might consider staying with us."

Bella threw her hands up in the air in excitement right away.

Scarlet laughed and for a moment it felt as if we had left behind the world of worries and troubles in California. The only challenge and worry on my mind now consisted of my family.

Would they accept Scarlet just like Bella had?

I had a lot going on in the back of my mind. My enemies were still out there and I feared that we were still in a lot of danger and I needed to protect everyone I loved from my demons.

Was Christmas dinner going to end up in another explosion?

17

SCARLET

The next morning after our arrival in New York was the part
that started to give me extreme anxiety. Damien's penthouse
looked more like a mansion from the inside. The home I
had seen back in California was nothing compared to what
his home in New York was like.

We had spent the entire morning with Bella. I had seen a
completely different side of him when he was around her. I
kept thinking about the child I was carrying myself and all
the fears and doubts I had in my mind regarding the child
not being safe in Damien's world. When I looked up from
the huge marble-coated breakfast table I sat at with Damien
and his daughter Bella my eyes landed on him. He had Bella
in his lap and a stack of blueberry pancakes resting before
them on the table. Every time she wanted a bite he would
make one for her with the perfect amount of maple syrup.
Her eyes would light up. I saw the way he was treating her
and I couldn't help but want my child to have a father who
would set the world aside for them.

Damien had caught me looking at him from across the
table. My eyes landed in his emerald green ones and a smile

instantly spread across his face. He playfully winked at me as he spoke. "Are you excited about Christmas dinner?"

I gulped.

The anxiety rose in my body.

Before I could reply Bella threw her hands in the air and spoke. "Of course, we're all excited! Grandma and Grandpa are going to be there. Everyone will come together like one big happy family!" I couldn't help but laugh. Her words were full of innocence and I knew Damien was doing everything in his power to bring me closer to his family and make me a part of his life. I wanted him be happy around his family. I didn't want him to worry about me while he was back home and so I smiled at him and Bella as I spoke. "I feel the same way as Bella. I'm really excited to meet your family." I could see by the look on his face he was at peace. I noticed the way his eyes were glimmering and I knew it would all be worth it in the end.

When breakfast was done Bella jumped off of Damien's lap and one of the maids in the house escorted her to her room. She waved at me as she ran across the house leaving Damien and me in the dining room. Damien got up from his seat and walked toward me. He wrapped his arms around my body and snuggled up close to me. I turned my head and my lips instantly crashed into his. He gently placed his hand on the back of my head to support me as he bit my bottom lip.

When he moved away from me, he noticed the wide smile spread across my face and he spoke in a flirty tone. "Someone looks really happy?"

I nodded my head at him as I spoke. "Of course I am, Damien. This is a side of you I never expected to see. I just want you to know I really appreciate you inviting me into your home and trying so hard to include me in your family. I know its hard for you to open up to anyone right away."

He cut me off before I could go on. My heart skipped a beat and a small scream escaped my lips as he pulled me up in his arms with one swift motion. Once I was in his arms he looked down at me and before I knew it his lips crashed into mine again. As he slowly pulled away he made sure to keep my bottom lip between his teeth as he stared into my eyes.

Once he let go of my lips, he whispered over to me as he carried me across the home. I focused on his words. "You never ever have to thank me for anything Scarlet. Always remember that."

He pushed the door to his bedroom open with one push of his leg; and as soon as he stepped inside, he threw me onto the bed. A smile spread across my face as he leaned over me and began to kiss me. I grabbed onto his shoulders and pulled him toward me. In the moment I wanted nothing more than to be with him but he stepped back slowly making me want him more.

He winked over to me as he pulled away from me and I acted grumpy as I scrunched up my nose and spoke. "That's not fair. You're just abandoning me?"

He shook his head at me and began to walk toward the huge walk in closet in the corner of the room. He pointed and yelled, "Stay there and don't move," before he walked into the closet.

I felt the heavy dominant side of his coming back as I remained on the bed and watched him from a distance.

After a few seconds passed he walked back out with what looked to be a new dress. He unzipped the packing and my eyes widened. He was holding a full-length black colored slim fitted dress in his hands. He pointed toward me once again and spoke. "I'm going to have to leave you until this evening. I need to prepare for dinner, but when I see you tonight, you better be wearing this."

He took a step forward. My heart skipped a beat as he grabbed me by my throat and pushed me further into the mattress. His hold got stronger with me. He made sure to tilt my head upwards and before I had the chance to even react his lips collided with mine again. He didn't let go of my throat. His hand moved toward the zipper of my jeans and he pushed his hand inside my jeans. My heart skipped a beat as his fingers brushed up against my clit. I couldn't even moan because of his hold on my throat. My eyes rolled to the back of my head.

He moved his mouth slowly to the side of my face. His teeth grazed my earlobe before whispering, "After you meet my family you better be prepared to scream at the top of your lungs tonight."

My body tingled. Every part of me wanted to push him closer to me and wrap my legs around his lower body, allowing him to make me scream as he took control perfectly. He pulled himself away from me, his hand moved out of my jeans and he pushed me toward the bed, he knelt down and moved a loose strand of hair from my eyes as he placed a gentle kiss upon my forehead as he spoke. "Take care princess and I'll see you at dinner."

My heart fluttered at how he could be dominant yet show his softer side as well.

Once Damien was gone, the rest of my day was spent in the room. Damien had left with Bella and they were apparently picking his brother up from the airport from what I heard him say. I rested my head on one of the pillows in his bed, and instantly, I felt sleep taking over my body. The past few weeks had been hectic, one after the other, and I felt like I could finally sleep in peace. My eyes fell shut and I drifted off to sleep.

I had no idea how much time had passed when I heard a familiar high-pitched sound piercing through my ears. My eyelids felt heavy. I slowly opened my eyes and my heart skipped a beat when I came face to face with Bella. She was on top of the bed and her face was just merely inches away from me as she yelled in my face. "Scarlet! You have to get up! Everyone is almost here! You can't be late. They're all waiting to meet you!"

I couldn't help but smile at the amount of excitement and energy pouring out of the little girl's body. But as she woke me up and my eyes lingered on the clock on the wall my heart skipped a beat. I couldn't believe I had actually slept for over five hours and it was already almost time for dinner. I pushed myself up against the headboard of the bed and came face to face with Bella. My eyes landed on the beautiful bright pink colored dress she was wearing. It had flowers stitched along the neckline reaching down to her knees. Her hair was pulled back by a matching pink hairband and her shoes went with her outfit too. I smiled brightly at her as I spoke. "Oh my you look so beautiful. I love your dress Bella!"

I watched as her eyes instantly lit up in the moment. She jumped up on the bed and landed in my lap as she spoke loudly.

"I know right! It was a surprise from Daddy. He always brings me the best presents."

Bella turned her head to the side of the room and her eyes landed on the black dress Damien had left out for me, she turned to face me again and spoke, "I'm guessing Daddy got you a dress too! Oh, I can't wait to see you in it. You know Daddy never really brought anyone home ever since mommy left. I'm really glad he chose to let you meet me because now we can twin and wear the same dresses!"

Before I could say anything at all the girl jumped off of the bed and hurried toward the main door. She lingered by the door for a moment and spoke to me once again.

"Please hurry and get ready. I really want you to meet everyone!"

I laughed at the beauty and energy the girl brought into the room. I pulled myself out of bed and gave her a firm nod. "I'm going to get ready as fast as I can and then I'll be right there with you!"

She nodded her head at me as she told me to hurry up as everyone had started to arrive. Bella hurried out of the room closing the door behind her. As soon as she was gone, I hurried toward the dress on the chair by the door. I had never gotten ready faster in my life. Once I was done, I started staring at myself in the large wall-sized mirror in Damien's room.

The dress he had bought me fit my body like a glove. It reached down to my feet and he had paired it with a golden chain. My hair was still a little damp from the shower I had taken that morning as the ends looked a little curly reaching down to my shoulders. I smiled to myself before I took a deep breath and prepared to step out of the room. I wondered if his family would even like me, if I would fit into their lifestyle or if I would stand out like a sore thumb. I knew stepping out of the door was the only way to answer my questions. So I pushed myself to go ahead and do that.

As I made my way through the hallway, I stood outside the large dinning room for a few seconds collecting my thoughts. I could hear muffled voices in the distance and Bella's laughs would occasionally spread into the room.

I drew in a deep breath before I finally stepped into the room. A large chandelier was glistening above the dining table and plates had been set in front of seats. Just when I entered the room my eyes landed on Damien first. He was the only one who stood up with a glass of wine in his hand. A smile was painted upon his face. He was wearing a white dress shirt with the first two buttons open. He turned to face me and instantly I watched as his face lit up. An old woman was sitting next to him. A glass of wine was placed near her too. Her hair had faded into a light shade of grey. Pearls were hanging from her neck and she was wearing a ghostly white blouse. Her hand was held by an older man. They both looked like they were in their late sixties. Bella was sitting in the man's lap. As I entered the room Damien instantly gestured toward me and spoke causing everyone's attention to me.

"Ah..finally Scarlet!"

I walked toward him and he wrapped his arm around my waist pulling me closer to him. My cheeks flushed in a bright shade of pink when he placed a small kiss on my cheek and spoke. "Ma, Pa this is Scarlet...Scarlet the duo that raised me to be the man I am today."

He gestured between the three of us and I moved forward to shake hands with his parents. His mother had Damien's eyes while his father's were a darker shade of black. His mother was the first to speak up and her words brought me a sense of comfort.

"Scarlet, it's lovely to finally meet the woman my son will not stop talking about."

His father nodded and I couldn't help but smile.

I spoke in a gentle and low tone addressing them. "It's a

pleasure for me to meet you both. You've done an extraordinary job with raising your son."

She brushed off what I said as she laughed between the words that left her mouth.

"Oh please! Us women know just how much anger my sons and my husband have inside of them."

She winked at me and I felt at ease. The meeting was going much better than I had ever expected.

Damien pulled open a chair next to his mother for me. Just as I was about to sit down the sound of heavy footsteps filled the room. I turned toward the main door of the dining room wondering who it was that had entered the room. Damien was still standing behind me. A taller figure came into the room, and it was as if I couldn't believe my eyes.

For a moment I thought I was seeing things.

Before me, there he was, standing by the door was the man I once allowed to break my heart. Tears gathered in my eyes. He looked older, more sober. His once all dark black hair was turning grey. His brown coffee tinted eyes landed on mine and he seemed just as shocked to see me as I was him.

Damien moved from behind me. He gestured toward the man I had once given my heart to as he spoke. "Ah you're finally here! Scarlet, meet my elder brother Marcus!"

It felt as if my heart had shattered all over again. I flashed back to the day the man stood before me completely broke my heart.

I couldn't hold it inside me anymore. My voice cracked as I spoke. "What....what the hell are you doing here?!"

18

DAMIEN

As soon as Marcus entered the room, I noticed an instant shift in Scarlet's behavior. She stiffened up. Her back faced me and yet I still felt the way she had gone cold. The room went silent for a mere moment. I pointed toward my brother. The man who had been there for me all throughout my life and the reaction I had gathered from Scarlet made me feel like I was standing next to a woman I didn't know. This wasn't the Scarlet I had fallen in love with.

Her voice echoed in the room. She rushed toward Marcus. Her voice was wavering. For a moment it felt as if time had slowed down. I had made it clear to Scarlet that my family came before anyone else. For a moment I couldn't believe she could be so openly disrespectful to my brother in front of the rest of my family. I couldn't stand by and watch her tear my reputation to shreds.

As Scarlet stomped toward Marcus, she raised her voice once again. I could see my mother's eyes wide with surprise. She yelled directly at Marcus once again. "I asked you something! What the hell are you doing here?"

My brother looked just as shocked. He didn't say a word

back. I knew that I needed to step up. This was my family and no one was allowed to step into my home and raise their voice at them. In the moment anger took over my body fully. I rushed toward Scarlet. She turned to face me and I could see tears filling her eyes.

In the moment my anger had taken over me. I yelled. The room went silent. My voice echoed in the room as I grabbed Scarlet by the arm. My grip on her was tight. It was too tight for her own good as the hurtful words left my mouth in an instant clashing with her conscious. "What the hell do you think you're doing?"

I moved forward. She took a step back but I wouldn't let go of her hand. She tried to pull away from me but in the moment my judgment had been clouded by anger. "Don't you ever speak to the people I love in this manner again!"

Tears streamed down her face. She pulled her hand away from me but I refused to let go until her words broke through the cloud of my judgment. "Damien.....you're hurting me."

In that moment, my eyes moved toward Marcus. He moved forward and pushed me out of the way. My grip loosened on Scarlet and before I had the chance to understand what was going on Scarlet had run out of the dining room. I turned toward Marcus. He approached me and raised his voice. "Damien, you really should not have done that."

My eyes widened. I didn't know what he was talking about. I had just protected him from disrespect. I stared at him in disbelief as I spoke with the anger still rising in my chest. "Did you hear the way she was speaking to you Marcus?"

He placed his hand on my shoulder gently as he tried to calm me down and spoke in a gentle tone. "Damien.....there is a lot you don't know about. She had every right to speak to me in that manner. She actually went easy on me considering our past."

Before I even had the chance to say anything at all I heard my mother's voice from the background. "Boys, I'm going to leave you two alone."

She grabbed Bella's hand and before I knew it my parents had left the room. Bella wanted to say something to me. I could see it in her eyes but she quietly took my mother's hand and left.

I turned to Marcus once it was just the two of us and spoke. "Can you please tell me what the hell is going on? I feel like I am losing my mind over here."

Marcus gestured toward the door Scarlet had just stormed out of. He took a deep breath before he spoke. "Damien, Scarlet, and I have a history."

Before he could even go on, my eyes widened. I couldn't believe what he was saying. For a moment I wanted to pinch myself. This couldn't be real. I raised my eyebrows as I spoke with disbelief lingering in my tone. "What kind of a history are you talking about?"

He sighed almost as if it was hard for him to put into words what he wanted to say to me. There was a moment of silence between the two of us. "Damien, Scarlet came into my life at a point when I wasn't myself. I didn't know what I wanted and I used her. I kept her on the sidelines of my life until the day I broke her heart."

I took a deep breath. A part of me could not believe what was happening to me. I stared at him and I knew my brother was telling the truth. This wasn't a joke or a prank. He was really telling me what happened. I spoke up confused more than ever. "When did this even happen? How did I miss it? And why the hell did you not say anything at all before?"

He sighed. His eyes refused to land on mine almost as if

he was ashamed. It took him a moment. "Damien I'm not going to tell you the details. I believe that it's her story to tell but all I am going to say to you is that if you lose her, it will be the biggest mistake of your life."

He paused before he went on. "I broke her heart. Don't you do the same."

When the events began to click back in my mind I felt my heart dropping. I thought back to the moment I had held on to her with my grip tightening her arm by the second. The image of tears lingering in her eyes came back to me and everything started to come together. It all came crashing down on me at once and I looked up at Marcus as I ran my fingers through my hair while the words left my mouth.

"Marcus, what have I done? Do you think it's too late to fix it now?"

Marcus squeezed my shoulder with his hand as he spoke. "Come on. Let's go find her. We both have some serious apologizing to do."

I sighed. A part of me wondered if this was the end. If she had finally given up on me. All the negative thoughts started raining down on me. Marcus took the lead. I followed him and I realized I had no idea where she would even be.

I spoke to Marcus with more fear washing over my body. "I don't even know where she went and for sure if security was following her since we were all supposed to be eating dinner now at home. How are we going to find her? It's New York. She could be anywhere after all."

I was ready to call security and ask them if they still had eyes on her but Marcus waved me off as he spoke. "I know exactly where she went. Follow me."

The whole car ride between us was quiet. I tried again

and again to ask him more about the situation, but Marcus kept telling me to trust Scarlet. I decided to follow his lead. I had already done enough and I just hoped she would forgive me even when she had seen the worst side of me. I promised Scarlet I would protect her from the world but in the moment I was the monster. I was the one she needed protection from.

I was pulled out of my thoughts when I realized Marcus gestured toward the New York subway. I couldn't remember the last time I had gone into a subway.

I raised my eyebrow. "Why do you want me to go into the Subway?"

I had never taken the subway for anyone before but when it came to Scarlet it seemed that there was no limit I wouldn't cross to get her back.

I could see a sense of sadness lingering in his eyes as he spoke. "This is where I broke her heart."

In the moment even though he was my brother I felt a sense of hatred wash over me. I couldn't help but be angry at him for ever hurting Scarlet.

I decided to stay focused on the situation.

We went into the subway and I could feel my skin crawling at every second with people bumping into my shoulders and the stench of alcohol and sweat mixed together spreading across the congested area. I took a deep breath and followed Marcus through the crowds of people. We walked to the end of the subway and I noticed that he stopped. His back was turned toward me and he was facing a bench in the left corner. I walked over to him and looked over his shoulder. My eyes landed on her and for a moment my heart shattered to pieces.

She sat in the left corner of the subway alone on a bench. Her head was tilted downwards, and loose strands of her blonde hair were falling over her face. I could instantly tell that she had been crying. I was grateful of the fact that a hoodie was draped over her body and she was wearing sweats. At least she was not still in heels and a gown.

I was on my way toward her and just as I took a step, Marcus reached forward and grabbed me by the arm.

He stopped me in my step as he spoke. "Damien, let me deal with this first."

Anger washed over my body. A part of me believed that Scarlet was my responsibility and watching someone say they would manage the heartache I caused struck me. I wanted to stay and fight for her. When I turned to face Marcus and saw the look in his eyes, I knew that he meant what he said. At the moment he needed me to step aside. For the sake of Scarlet, I decided to listen to him and put my own ego aside.

I offered him a firm nod as I spoke before I walked the other way. "You better take care of her."

I knew this was the moment that would either make us or break us once and for all.

19

———

SCARLET

The subway was cold. I could hear the trains screeching in the distance and children crying accompanied by heavy footsteps of people passing by. My head was held in my hands and I was trying to get myself to start breathing normally once again. I sighed as I tried my best not to feel anything at all but I kept replaying the moment I had seen Marcus in the dining room. The way he looked at me after all these years. He was the last person I ever expected to see. I still couldn't believe my eyes.

I saw Damien as a man who would protect me no matter what. I still couldn't forget the first time I had met him and the way he saved me. He had even almost taken a bullet for me. He promised me he would do everything in his power to keep me safe but he had done the exact opposite. I remembered the way he grabbed me. The flash of anger in his eyes. When I looked at him, I didn't see the man I loved, but rather a completely different person.

My hands were shaking with anger. My heart skipped a beat. I instantly looked up when I felt that someone had touched my shoulder. All my defenses came into play, I was very close to smacking the person over the head. When I turned my head, my eyes instantly met Marcus's. My body went numb. I wanted to speak, move, or react but I was frozen in place. A part of my brain still hadn't registered that Marcus was back in my life after all of the pain he caused me.

I didn't even get the chance to say anything. He spoke before I could even fully react. "Scarlet...can we please talk? I promise no one will hurt you or be loud. I just want to talk to you."

He knelt down until he was at my level while I was sitting on the bench. He was way taller than me. The subway still bustling with people in the background. I tried my best not to show any weakness. I gulped and pushed myself to speak up. "I really don't want anything to do with you Marcus or your brother for that matter. I am done with all of you. Please just let me be."

I couldn't help it. My voice cracked as I spoke. The tears already lined my eyes and Marcus stayed in his place. I wanted to get up and leave him there but it felt like I couldn't move.

He kept his eyes on me. "I know I hurt you a lot and if I apologize for the rest of my life it won't be enough. I just want you to know I broke your heart because I was not ready for a relationship. I kept you in the shadows and never told you anything about me. Scarlet, I was a very shitty person to you but I can honestly say from the bottom of my heart I beg you to please not take the pain I caused you out on my brother. Don't punish him for my mistakes."

It felt like the apology came after it was too late. Marcus was the first man I trusted and he kept me in the shadows. Our entire relationship was a secret and when I asked for more he broke things off with me. This wasn't the worst part. A while later I found out he had been cheating on me the entire time. No one had ever made me feel so bad about myself before.

I sighed. I could see by the look on his face that he was being genuine with every word that left his mouth. For a long moment, there was silence between the two of us. He waited for me to say something but when I refused to do so he gestured toward the other corner of the subway where people were passing by and spoke. "I know what he did to you back there was wrong. Damien loves you Scarlet. He had no idea what the situation between the two of us was. He brought you into his home and you met his daughter. Scarlet I have never seen him doing anything like this for a woman before. He really is trying. It's just that his ex-wife betrayed him before and you are the first woman he has let into his life so closely since then. I may not have been the one for you but he is. And he really regrets what he did. Please, can you just give him the chance to speak to you?"

My eyes lingered in the other corner and I could see him standing there. He refused to even look up. He looked defeated and his head was held low. I had never seen him in this state. I took a deep breath as I looked between Marcus and him.

For the sake of the unborn child I was carrying in my belly and the feelings I had for Damien, I would speak to him. I nodded my head at him letting him know that I would allow him to speak to me. Marcus instantly jumped to his feet. He thanked me with everything in him as he rushed toward Damien.

I moved my eyes away from them and focused my gaze back on the floor. A few seconds passed before a familiar voice brushed through my ears. "Scarlet?"

I looked up and my eyes landed on him.

He looked like a mess. His hair was loose and falling over his eyes, his hands tucked into the pockets of his winter coat, and his eyes had gone red almost as if he had been crying.

He gestured toward the exit as he spoke once again. "If it's okay with you, can we talk in a more private place?"

I shook my head. "I think I'm better off here. Say whatever you want, Damien."

I knew that I wasn't expressing any emotions to him. My voice was plain. I was holding back my tears and trying my best to keep everything inside.

He nodded and did not argue with me at all. I moved a little to the right making room for him to sit next to me and he did so immediately.

He clasped his hands together as he spoke. "I could say I'm sorry but I know that sorry will not make up for the pain I have caused you."

I stayed quiet as he went on.

"I had no idea at the moment that you had history with my brother. If I would have known I would have stood by your side because what he did to you was wrong. I don't know the details but I know he hurt you."

He took a pause and I spoke before he had the chance to. "He kept me like a secret. He used me for his own gain and then broke my heart." I turned to face Damien and looked him dead in the eyes as the rest of the words left my mouth. "What if you do the same to me?'

I watched as the fear of what I said flashed before his eyes and he instantly began to shake his head. He did not dare to reach for my hands as he spoke. "I know right now you hate me and you have every right to do so but I promise you that everything I have done for you I have done with a clear heart. You are the woman I want to spend the rest of my life with and I know my anger is my biggest vice but I am trying my best to work on it. I really love you from the bottom of my heart."

I could see tears in his eyes. I sighed. I didn't know what to feel. In that moment the words just fell from my mouth. "Do you think if I give you another chance you won't hurt me like this again?"

Damien turned to face me. All of his attention was focused on me as he spoke. "Scarlet, this is love. You will end up hurting me some day and I will hurt you too. But we will also love each other more than ever. And when things go wrong and we make mistakes you will know that I will be there for you every single time and I will never hide you from the world or abandon you."

The tears began to pour from my eyes. The hurt had started to fade away and through the mask and all the walls he had put up, I could finally see Damien for who he really was.

He was a man who loved with an open heart and was not afraid of admitting when he made a mistake. He wouldn't push me away. Instead, he was the first person to hold me close and come to me even when I refused to see him. He took a small pause before he spoke again. "Scarlet, please let's go back home. Everyone is waiting and it's freezing out here. Let's have a nice dinner and let me make all of this up to you. If you don't want Marcus to join, I will be okay with that. I can ask him to leave and you will never have to see him again.'

I sighed. I knew he was trying his best to make things right but deep inside I also knew that if I wanted things to work with Damien fully I would have to let go of my past with Marcus. He had apologized and time had passed. The wounds healed. It was time to move forward. My eyes lingered toward the other side and I could see Marcus waiting by the wall for us to finish talking.

Damien waited for my reply and I finally allowed my eyes to meet with his as I spoke. "I think it is time for all of us to leave the past in the past. Let's just go back and eat something."

I had merely just stood up when Damien grabbed me by the waist and pulled me toward him. I spun into his arms and just as I looked up with shock in my eyes he spoke in a gentle yet possessive manner.

"Can I kiss you?" he asked.

I nodded. He bent down instantly and his lips crashed into mine right away. In that moment, we did not care where we were or who was watching. All that mattered was that we were together.

After he moved his lips away from mine, he gently kissed my cheek. I felt my face burning up a little bit. He took my hand into his as we headed toward the stairs of the subway. Marcus, who was following behind us and giving us some space, tapped me on the shoulder. He asked if I could speak to him for a moment, so I told Damien to proceed while I walked slower next to Marcus.

As soon as Damien was a little out of sight Marcus spoke up in a low tone as if he was being cautious that Damien might hear him. "Scarlet listen up, so. Damien's birthday is in a few days and he never really celebrates but this time I thought maybe we should do something since the whole family is together and we can all use a little break. Not to mention it's not safe for any of us to be out in the streets like this."

I nodded. An idea popped into the back of my mind. "How about we throw him a surprise birthday party? We can invite only close family and friends for safety purposes and it can be a nice way for him to relax."

I looked over at him and I knew he was on my side too. I only prayed for the birthday to go on without any drama or explosions.

It was Damien's life, who was I kidding? A part of me expected the drama that would soon follow.

20

DAMIEN

THE NEXT MORNING HAD BEEN VERY ODD. SCARLET AND Marcus had practically kicked Bella and me out of the home in New York and onto the streets claiming that Bella needed to shop. I couldn't understand why all of us couldn't go together but in the moment I had decided to trust Scarlet. Besides Bella and I needed quality time. It had been a while since we spent time together.

As the day had slowly started to come to an end and Karl placed the multiple shopping bags in the back of the car, Bella turned to me. I could see a wide smile spread across her face as she spoke. "Are you excited Daddy?"

As soon as I saw the expression on her face, I knew that something was off. I turned to face her and raised my eyebrow. "Excited for what exactly?"

I tried to use a serious tone of voice so she would scramble and spill the truth of whatever she was hiding from me but the girl seemed to be keeping everything she knew zipped. She ignored me as she turned to Karl whose eyes were fixed on the road. "Karl! Let's go back home!"

As the sun had started to set in the distance and the sky was roaring with clouds I tried my best to get Bella to tell me if she was keeping a secret but she refused. Before I knew it, we had reached home. As soon as the car entered though the gates of the complex I looked around for any clues but everything seemed normal and in place. By the time we reached the front door of the mansion, I had given up. I felt exhausted from carrying Bella around the streets of New York. A part of me just wanted to step inside, go to my bedroom, and pass out.

As soon as the front doors to the house opened up my heart dropped down to my stomach. Bella screeched in the background and noise echoed throughout the whole house. Before my eyes, the whole house was covered with people from my family and friends I had grown up with, faces I had not seen in a while, and almost all of them were screaming Happy Birthday in my face. For a moment, I was too surprised even to speak. My eyes landed on Scarlet. She was standing in the middle of the crowd with a huge cake in her hand and candles lighting up the dark room.

She had a smile spread across her face. A red-colored glistening gown was splendidly placed upon her body as she made her way toward me. Everyone else in the room disappeared into the distance. My eyes remained fixed only on her and as soon as she walked over to me I bent down and blew all of the candles out one by one.

Sounds of applause spread through the room. Everyone was cheering. Scarlet handed the cake to Marcus, who wished me a happy birthday and as soon as her hands were free, I grabbed her by her lower waist. I pulled her body toward me and a giggle escaped her lips. She was about to say something but I pulled her into a small hug knowing there were too many people around and we could not kiss in the moment.

As I slowly let go of her, she smiled over at me as she spoke. "So did you like the surprise?"

My heart was full of gratitude at the moment. My grip tightened on her as I replied in a hushed tone. People passing by were wishing me a happy birthday but my eyes remained fixed on her throughout the entire party. "No one has ever done anything like this for me Scarlet. You have no idea how grateful I am for you."

She gestured toward everyone at the party as she spoke. "Come on. I couldn't have done it without the help of everyone, especially Marcus."

My eyes lingered over on Marcus who was speaking to one of our cousins. He turned to face me and even with the distance between us, he raised his glass of champagne toward me. I nodded. It was an exchange of thank you's.

I knew the party was going on in the distance but my eyes remained fixed on Scarlet. She raised her eyebrow at me in a surprised manner as she spoke. "Are you okay honey?"

I shook my head. My eyes were directly focused on hers. I reached for her arm and once I had grabbed her, I began to make my way through the party guests. People had tried to stop me in between but I simply shrugged them off with a smile on my face. I could hear the sound of Scarlet's heels clicking behind me as she threw questions in the air about why we had left the party behind but I refused to reply to her as we carried on moving toward the hallway leading to the bedrooms.

I could hear the party music in the distance. As soon as I opened the door to my bedroom I made sure to slam it right behind me. I twisted the lock on the door and Scarlet stood behind me. She spoke up once again, "Can you please explain why we just ran away from a party I worked my ass off for?"

I turned around and offered her my hand. She rolled her eyes as she placed her hand in mine. In one swift motion, I pulled her toward me. Her back was now pressed against the bedroom door and her eyes widened when I made sure to step so close to her that there was merely an inch between us. Her heart skipped a beat as I spoke with my lips lingering over hers for a small moment.

"I'm thanking you for the party, princess."

Before she knew it my lips were on hers, her arms were wrapped around my shoulders. I pushed her body upwards until she was in my lap and my right hand gripped her thigh tightly. I had her pinned to the door as my kisses trailed down her neck toward her breasts. Her dress had an eloquent cut between her breasts and I used it to my advantage. She tilted her head upwards and a moan escaped her lips as I reached for the back of her dress with my left hand, and within seconds, the garment was on the floor.

She looked up at me and I could see the same fire in her eyes. Lust came between the two of us.

I had her in my arms as I moved toward the bed without letting go of her lips from between my teeth for even a single moment. As I threw her body onto my bed, I stared at her beautiful figure laid out upon my silk sheets for a moment before I brushed my own shirt over my neck and threw it across the room. The party music had started to dull away into the background.

I made sure to carefully split Scarlet's legs open before me. My fingers ran over her clit a few times as my hands tightened upon her thong and moans escaped her lips. Her neck and chest were already covered in purple bruises, mine.

I made sure to dig three fingers deep inside of her and as I heard her scream I pulled them out before pushing them inside of her once again. Her nails were digging into my skin, pain mixed with pleasure was what it was. Just as my fingers started to move in and out of her faster and faster her legs began to shake. She was near climax when I stopped all at once and brought my fingers filled with her white fluid to my face and I licked them right before her eyes.

Her eyes rolled to the back of her head as her body wanted more. A wicked smile appeared upon my lips as I brought my face closer to her ear. I grabbed her head from the back of her hair as I whispered to her.

"You want me to keep going?" She was out of breath, her chest was heaving up and down, she nodded her head and my grip tightened on her hair as I yanked her head closer to me and spoke once again. "Beg for it. Beg for me."

The look in her eyes changed. She pushed herself closer to me as the words escaped her mouth in mere whispers. "Please...Damien. I need you, please."

I was on my knees with her legs spread before me. She was begging for me as I brought my left hand toward her lips. My thumb pressed down on her bottom lip before I pushed it inside her mouth. She looked up at me with innocence dripping in her eyes as she sucked on my thumb before I pulled it out of her mouth and pushed her down on the bed.

I was between her legs. She gripped on to my shoulders as I placed myself before her clit. I lifted her legs upwards until her ankles were resting on my shoulders. I whispered over to her, "You ready baby?"

She looked up at me and as soon as the "yes" escaped her mouth, I pushed my hard throbbing member inside of her. Pushing through her walls as moans escaped her mouth. I made sure to start off slow before I started to speed up. Her eyes rolled to the back of her head. Her grip tightened on me until I finally came inside her.

My body fell next to hers and I pulled her close as both of our breaths were heaving up and down.

Scarlet looked over at me and spoke briefly after catching her breath. "Damn, that was the best thank you I have ever gotten."

Her cheeks were flushed in a light shade of pink. I smiled as I ran my fingers over the side of her face tracing her cheeks before I replied. "Come on let's clean ourselves up. We have a party to get back to."

By the time we made it out of the bedroom door, the party was full of half-drunk rich people dancing around. The cake was gone and Champagne was being passed around at every second. I smiled as I looked around the room. I couldn't help but feel glad that even after all the risks I had taken to keep Scarlet in my life, every part of me knew I had made the right choice.

I was about to turn to Marcus who was approaching me and thank him in person when, suddenly, I felt a tight grip on my shoulder from behind. My guard was immediately up. I turned around instantly and someone I thought I would never see again was standing so close to me I could feel his breath upon my skin as he spoke. Shivers ran down my spine, and memories of the attacks flooded back to me as his words hit me at once.

"Nice party Damien...."

I heard Marcus yelling in the distance, he had seen

exactly what I feared too. His words echoed in the distance. "Security! Security!"

It was too late. The man in front of me pointed upwards, and a smirk was placed on his face. I could hear sirens in the distance. I could feel the security on its way with the sounds of their heavy boots on the ground. I already knew it was too late. I looked up and my eyes landed on the huge chandelier taking up almost half of the room with diamonds hanging from it. My eyes landed on Scarlet and Marcus who were both under the chandelier. I didn't wait a second before I screamed.

"Get out of the way! Move! It's going to..."

I couldn't continue, and before I knew it Marcus grabbed Scarlet by the arm and pushed her out of the way. In seconds the giant chandelier collapsed to the ground. My body hit the tiles below me. I heard screams erupting in the air and glass cracking upon the tiles.

I had hit my head directly on a piece of glass. I could feel the side of my face starting to get damp with blood. Security was flooding into the room, and chaos had erupted all around. Even when I was almost out of energy after being knocked down, I knew I couldn't let the enemy from my past, Oliver, get away. I had to end the attacks for the sake of Scarlet and my daughter. I needed to end it for all.

I pushed myself to my feet and began to run between the people who had all collapsed on the ground. I could hear women screaming. Glasses were broken, pieces of the chandelier crunched under my feet as I limped toward the exit where the man with dark grey hair was running toward. I took a deep breath before I reached for the gun in the back of my belt. I heard screams around me at the sight of the gun. From the corner of my eye, I could see Scarlet. She sat next to Marcus. Her eyes were fixed at what I was about to do.

I aimed at his shoulder and without thinking twice, I pressed the trigger.

Boom.

21

———

SCARLET

I COULD STILL HEAR THE SOUND OF THE GUNSHOT. IT WAS ringing in the back of my head. I still couldn't push the image out of my mind. Something had taken over Damien. I remembered watching as he held the gun upwards and pulled the trigger with close to no remorse in his body.

The police were walking over the house. Three of the detectives had taken the man with grey hair away. Blood was still splattered on the ground. I sat in the corner. I was pushed out of my thoughts when Damien's voice spread across the hall with shattered glass still on the ground.

"How the hell did he get inside? What was the security I paid thousands of dollars to doing?!"

He hadn't calmed down. Blood was still dripping from his face. Marcus was trying to get the situation with the cops under control as he gave them a statement. I walked over to Damien and spoke in the most gentle manner possible. "Damien, you're bleeding. Can you please listen to the nurse and get cleaned up first?"

He turned around and I could see something flashing in

his eyes, anger. "Can you please get the hell away from me?! Didn't you just see what happened?!"

I ignored the outburst but just as I tried to reach for his arm he pushed me away causing my body to falter backward before I gained balance again and he yelled again. "I swear to God, sometimes you don't even see what is going on! Just stay the hell away from me! Someone get her out of here before I lose my mind and kick her out!"

Tears formed in my eyes as I looked at him. The man I fell in love with, was not there. All I saw was anger as he turned his back on me and yelled at the men who seemed to be with the security.

"I need an answer! How the hell could you let this happen? Who was at the door? Who let him in!"

I took a step closer to him and he turned to me again as he yelled with his eyes refusing to meet mine.

"Dammit Scarlet! Get the hell away from me. I can't deal with you right now. Please just go! For once in your life just listen to me and get the hell away!"

I felt fear rising in my body. Marcus approached me and spoke to me in a calm manner. "Scarlet, give him some time to cool down and deal with the situation. Come on let's go."

He escorted me to Damien's bedroom and as soon as I was inside I felt like I was moments away from breaking down.

Marcus wrapped his arms around me and hugged me, and the words just fell from my mouth. "Why does he do that? One moment he's so loving and the next he treats me like I'm nothing."

He sighed and while placing both hands on my shoulders he spoke. "The thing about Damien is that he is an amazing person until anyone he loves falls in danger. And then he just switches off all of his emotions in an effort to protect the people he loves. Sometimes he ends up hurting them too. Give him some time. He will come to his senses."

I nodded, I still heard the sirens. "What is going to happen? With the police and everything?"

Marcus spoke up instantly, "Well, that man you saw his name is Oliver and he was after Damien's company for a while. I think the last time Damien got him arrested was a few weeks ago but you know money and contacts can get anyone released. What matters now is that he will be behind bars for the rest of his life. So don't worry he's gone for good."

I nodded my head. I was about to ask him more when Marcus and I heard a knock on the door. Marcus pulled the door open and there he was, Damien. He seemed more calm now. He gestured for Marcus to leave us alone in the room. I stepped back when Damien stepped into the room. Blood stains were still visible on his face and his shirt. For a moment silence spread between the two of us. I turned away from him. I couldn't even look at him as he spoke.

"I did it again didn't I?'

I nodded my head in disappointment as I spoke in a mere whisper. "You mean you let your anger out on me and treated me like shit again? Yes Damien. Yes you did."

He walked over to me slowly and stopped a few inches away from me as he spoke. "Scarlet, in the moment, when I saw someone I thought I put away for good, every red warning sign flashed in my mind. I had to protect you. You have to believe that I was just as blindsided as you or anyone else. The fact that he got through security...I felt helpless."

I cut him off before he could go on. "You shot him Damien. I just watched a man I love shoot someone!"

Damien raised his voice this time in defense. He reached for my hand and placed it upon my belly as he spoke. "Yes I shot him! I would do it a hundred times over because Scarlet in the moment, the chandelier fell all I could think about was you, my unborn child, the rest of my family and friends, and what if, what if you were under the chandelier? I would have lost you both. I did what I did to protect the ones I love and I would do it all over again."

I broke down when I heard the words that left his mouth. My body fell onto his. He held me close to him as I whispered between the tears falling from my eyes.

"I'm tired Damien. I'm tired of the fighting and the hiding and all of this. I just want to have a normal life with you. That's all I want."

He ran his hands through my hair as he spoke. "You're safe now. It's all over. They're all gone. All the bad guys are gone."

I gripped onto him as my body started to break down. He put his hands on my shoulders as his eyes were staring directly back at me. "I'm going to go clean myself up. You stay here, okay. I'm just going to take a shower and then I'm all yours. We can stay in and watch a movie or do anything that will calm you down."

He wiped the tears from my eyes as he carried me in his arms toward the bed. He placed me down upon the sheets carefully as he placed a kiss on my forehead and spoke. "I can ask my mom to bring Bella back to the house and we can have a small family night?"

I nodded. A part of me was grateful that Damien's mother had taken Bella from the party early to her house knowing that the girl would have been in danger if she had stayed.

Just before Damien walked toward the bathroom he pointed toward my phone which was sitting on the dresser as he spoke. "By the way, you might want to take a look at your emails while I'm in the shower."

Before I could question him he was gone. I turned to grab my phone from the dresser and as I went through my emails. My eyes landed on one of the more recent ones that I had received and I froze in place.

I pinched myself for a moment. I couldn't believe what I saw. My eyes traced over the interview letter from one of the largest magazines in Paris and I felt like I was close to fainting.

I had dreamt of submitting my writing to the very magazine. It was one of my biggest goals and now I was staring at an opportunity of an interview with them for a senior article writer at their office.

I sat on the bed with tears in my eyes. I couldn't believe what I was looking back at. This couldn't be real. I waited for Damien before I broke the news to anyone at all. It took a while. Damien finally stepped out of the bathroom. His shirt was unbuttoned and his hair was still wet. He walked toward me and I instantly jumped up.

I had tears in my eyes as I screamed at him. "Damien, what the hell is this! How? How did this even happen? I never gave them my samples? I don't understand how my dream company just emailed me for an interview! Damien please explain to me how this happened or I'm going to lose my mind!"

A smirk appeared on his lips. He stepped closer to me as he spoke in a gentle tone. "I might or might not have sent your samples to them the day you told me you wanted to be a professional writer at their firm and all. I knew deep down you doubted yourself too much and you wouldn't go through with it even though you are one of the best writers I have ever met."

I couldn't believe the words that were spilling out of his mouth. I instantly jumped toward him causing him to stumble backward as I wrapped my arms around his body and pulled him closer to me instantly. A smile spread across his face as he placed a kiss upon my lips.

When he pulled his lips away from me for a moment he gestured toward my phone as he spoke. "Wait a minute, where exactly did they call you for the interview?"

I turned to the phone and spoke up right away as I remembered they had mentioned the location of the interview and the date in the email. "It's in Paris, Damien! Can you imagine?! Paris of all places! And it's just a week from now. They have provided me with a ticket and the hotel information...."

Before I could go on Damien cut me off. He placed a finger over my lips causing me to shut up as he spoke. "Nonsense, you're not flying anywhere commercial. You know there is a reason I have a private jet."

My eyes were wide. Before I could say anything at all he spoke up once again. "We're going to travel to Paris in style."

My mouth dropped open with shock as I repeated what he had just said to me. "Wait, what do you mean we? You're willing to come with me?"

He rolled his eyes at me as if I was a child who had just spoken some gibberish. He wrapped his arm around my shoulder as he spoke.

"Of course, I'm coming with you. It's Paris! The City of love. You think I'm going to let you go there alone?"

I guess we were going to Paris? I still couldn't believe it.

22

DAMIEN

"WHEN IS SHE GOING TO BE DONE?"

I was pulled out of my haze of thoughts by Bella's voice as it pierced through my ears. She was banging on the window in the small cafe by the Eiffel Tower we had chosen to sit in. Bella had joined us on the small vacation to Paris for Scarlet's interview. I sighed as I pointed toward the unfinished cup of hot chocolate placed in front of Bella and spoke in a stern tone as I tried to calm her down. "I'm sure she'll be here in a bit. Why don't you finish your drink. It's getting cold now."

We were trying our best to stay undercover and it was tough not being able to hold Scarlet in public and kiss her knowing I was still her boss and we had to keep things low-key.

She rolled her eyes at me as she carefully wrapped both her fingers around the mug of hot cocoa that was almost twice the size of her hands. My eyes drifted toward the view outside. I could see tourists bustling through the busy streets of Paris. Women were stopping at every corner for pictures and families were running around with joy spread across their faces. Bella and I were waiting at a small cafe with a beautiful view as Scarlet had left to the headquarters of one of the largest Fashion Magazines in business.

Scarlet had been clueless to the fact that the interview wasn't the only reason we had flown to Paris. I knew that we had been through a lot together, regardless of the fights, the misunderstandings as well as the dangers I had put her through she was the only woman who had decided to stay by my side. She treated my daughter like her own and she was carrying a child of mine as well.

I wanted nothing more than to have a child with Scarlet, and it had been circling in the back of my mind how she had wanted to put her career first too. She was one of the most beautiful writers I had ever seen but Scarlet lacked self-confidence. I knew the only way I could show her that she was worthy of being more than just a secretary at my office was to go ahead and submit the samples she had emailed me to read a while back.

I wanted Scarlet to be sure and completely happy with the decision to have a child with me. I didn't want her to regret not focusing on her career or letting her dreams go because of me. Even though the interview meant the world to Scarlet, I had my own surprises prepared for her in Paris. Now that Oliver who had been after my company had been caught and the weight of danger was lifted from my shoulders, it was time for me to focus on finally being able to hold hands with Scarlet in public and show the world the woman who had stolen my heart openly.

Before I could venture further and deeper into my thoughts about exactly what I had planned on the trip ahead for the two of us, I was once again jolted out of my thoughts by Bella's voice as it echoed through the cafe causing a few heads to turn from the tables around us as well.

"She's here! Finally! What took you so long?!"

My eyes instantly turned toward the door and I could see Scarlet walking toward her. She had a huge smile on her face as she opened both her arms and allowed Bella to fall within them. A laugh escaped my lips when I saw the way Bella was hugging Scarlet and after a few short moments, I decided to cut the sweet moment short as I spoke. "Okay, okay, that's enough. It's my turn to get a hug too."

Bella sighed in frustration as she gave up and moved away from Scarlet. I noticed that as soon as Scarlet turned toward me the smile on her face had loosely faltered. Like she had been pretending to be happy in front of Bella. I raised my eyebrow at her while I opened my arms. She gave me a quick side hug but she seemed twice as deflated and low on energy as compared to when we had dropped her at the interview.

Worry washed over my body. I spoke up making sure my eyes were directly focused on her. "Baby, is everything okay? Did the interview go well?"

She looked up at me but her gaze wavered away from me instantly as she spoke in a low tone. It was almost as if she didn't want Bella to hear what she was saying,

"Yes, I mean I think they're very demanding and they seem to have many options, but I tried my best so let's hope everything works out for the better."

Her tone had changed and I had noticed how she was trying to avoid any more questions regarding the interview. She turned to Bella as she spoke with excitement in her tone and even though she made it look like she was alright, I knew something was wrong.

I couldn't say anything in the moment as I heard her

speaking to Bella. "Bella, honey what do you think we should do first? Get some pictures near the Tower or get ice cream from that famous place I told you about around the corner from here?"

I knew that we needed to go but just as Scarlet was about to grab her coat from the chair next to her, and head out of the door with us, I grabbed her by the arm and pulled her backwards. She was caught by surprise in the given moment before she turned to face me and I spoke in a low tone.

"I know you're not okay Scarlet. Why don't you come back to the hotel with me and we can talk about the interview? Tory can take Bella out for some ice cream with Karl."

It was a given that whenever I traveled with my daughter the two people I trusted the most with her would always come along for situations where I would have an emergency meeting or something would happen.

Scarlet seemed to have a rather defeated look written all over her face. She was about to make some excuse to avoid whatever had happened during her interview, but I took a step toward her and placed both my hands gently on her shoulders. I made sure eyes were fixed on mine as I offered her a small smile and spoke to her in the calmest tone possible.

"Scarlet, honey, I know you're not okay and the more you avoid talking about whatever happened the worse you'll feel. Please just come back to the room. Talk to me. Tell me what you're feeling without any pressure."

I watched as a smile spread across her face right away. She gave me a small nod and I knew I needed to take Bella to Tory and Karl right away.

By the time we headed to the hotel room Scarlet had gone completely quiet. She wasn't even trying to make small talk on the way when Karl asked her about how she liked being in Paris. I knew something was awfully wrong with her, I had never seen her shutting down like this before.

I stayed silent until we were finally inside of the hotel room. The hotel was merely just a short drive from the Tower. We could see the lights of the Tower glistening from the hotel room every night. I watched as Scarlet slowly walked toward the large door leading to the balcony. She seemed to be staring out toward the glistening lights in the distance. I approached her slowly, her back was facing me, but she could see me in the reflection of the glass door. I pressed my body against her and placed small kisses on her shoulders.

A few moments passed in silence until she finally spoke up before I could ask her myself. "I don't think they're going to pick me, Damien. I'm sorry for the disappointment. I know you took time out of your tough schedule to bring me here and you tried. You tried your best for me."

Her voice trailed off almost as if she was about to cry. My heart skipped a beat for a moment. I took her by the hand slowly as I turned her around so that she could face me and when my eyes fell upon hers, I could see tear streaks lining her cheeks.

I wiped the tear stains from her face slowly and gently with my fingers as I spoke right away. "Hey, baby, come on. You never have to apologize to me for stuff like this. Everything I do for you is my choice and I would do a hundred times more than this for you."

I could see her trying to force a smile on her face. I gently kissed her forehead as I spoke up once again.

"As for the interview, honey this was the first try and we went big. The fact is that you got an interview without even knowing or trying hard. You had no idea about anything at all and I was the one who sent in your samples. Even if you don't get the job here you need to keep in mind that this is a gateway for you to keep trying. You have so much potential. People spend their whole lives trying to get noticed by magazines like these and you got so close."

I had to stop to take a deep breath. It felt like I had been talking forever. My eyes remained fixed on Scarlet, I could see she was finally trying to cool down a little bit.

I barely saw it coming when she moved forward in an instant and placed her lips upon mine. I closed my eyes as she began to kiss me slowly and she whispered under her breath while grabbing onto my button-up tightly.

"Just make me forget about today. Please."

I knew exactly what she wanted and I wasted no time.

I placed my hands under her thighs and instantly pulled her into my lap, she gasped all of a sudden but I didn't allow her to say anything as I kissed her roughly upon her lips right away. She was gripping my shoulders as I held her body in my arms. Scarlet lifted her head upwards and I instantly bit down on her neck. Her whole body shivered. My hands gripped her ass while I walked toward the marble countertop a few feet away from the balcony.

The sun had already set, and the Eiffel Tower glistened with tiny shining lights in the distance. I placed Scarlet on the countertop, her hair was loosely falling over her eyes. My hands gripped her top and I ripped the garment apart as a few buttons fell to the ground. I used one hand to take off her bra while my other hand pulled her panties down from beneath the black skirt she was wearing.

She was still holding onto my back as she placed a few kisses upon my chest. I looked over at her making sure to gaze into her eyes before I placed my right hand on her neck and pushed her down so she was lying down on her back with her legs dangling from the countertop. I knelt and began to lick her clit with both my hands holding her legs apart.

I could feel her body shaking. She was breathing deeply and moans had started to escape her mouth as I ran my tongue up and down upon her clit. I knew I had hit the spot when her legs began to shake. I smiled to myself and licked my lips before I pulled away from her.

Before she could say anything at all, I pulled her upwards instantly with her hands and as soon as she was up I pushed her down onto her knees before me as I grabbed a fist full of her hair. She looked up at me and blinked a few times looking as innocent as ever causing me to feel my boner within my pants.

I kept my eyes on her as I tugged at a fist full of her hair and spoke up in a rather demanding tone. "Get to work for Daddy."

I gestured toward the boner that was very much visible from my trousers and she nodded her head at me before she slowly began to take off my belt. My trousers fell to the ground and before I knew it she had taken my member out of my boxers. She wrapped her fingers around it before she took it into her mouth instantly.

My eyes rolled to the back of my head. Pleasure went through my whole body as she began to move her mouth. It was hitting the back of her throat every now and then and she refused to gag even once. I was amazed as she carried on until I felt myself letting go. I looked down at her with my eyes focused on her. I watched as she swallowed every last drop of the fluid that came out of me.

After she swallowed, I pulled her to her feet. A smile spread across her face as she spoke. "Was I okay?"

I pulled her closer to me and placed a kiss on her lips as

I replied right away, "You made me feel like my soul was on fire."

I could tell that she was proud of herself. I wasn't done with her yet. I gestured toward the master bathroom at the end of the hall and told her to get in the shower. I would be joining her soon.

I was on my way to the shower when I thought to check my phone in case I had received an important call.

My hand accidentally reached for Scarlet's phone which was placed next to mine. For a mere moment, my eyes lingered over the text message displayed on the screen and my heart dropped down to my stomach when I realized the text had been sent earlier in the evening and looked to be a part of a text chain.

"Scarlet, it was lovely seeing and meeting you. I haven't seen talent much like yourself in a while. I cannot wait to have you on board with the magazine. Waiting for your approval."

23

SCARLET

I COULD HEAR THE SHOWER RUNNING IN THE BATHROOM. My thoughts were scattered around in my mind. A part of me wanted to be honest with Damien and spill the secret I held inside me. The truth was that I had received an offer for my dream job. The happiness of the news stuck for a mere moment before the demons came crawling back and fears began to get the best of me. As soon as I had received the news, worries washed over me. Not only was I carrying a child but it wasn't just anyone's child. A part of me knew that the job came with the obligation of living in Paris for the first two years before I could go fully remote. Damien was not just any man who would or could move his whole life across the globe with the snap of his fingers. He was the CEO of a huge company, a businessman, and a father. I knew I couldn't ask for him to move to Paris for me and I didn't know if I could survive raising a child without him in a new country.

As much as I wanted the job, at the moment, I decided I was going to make a sacrifice for my unborn child and for the man I loved. I decided to tell him I didn't get an offer. He was doing everything in his power to be there for me and I felt the guilt rising up in the bottom of my stomach.

I was still standing in the bathroom when I heard his voice. He was calling out to me and I sighed as I grabbed the bathrobe that hung in the bathroom. I put the robe on and walked out of the bathroom.

As soon as my eyes landed on him I knew that something was wrong. He was siting at the edge of the bed with his hands clasped together and his eyes focused on the ground.

I walked up to him and spoke softly wondering what had caused his mood to flip so suddenly. "So you got the job didn't you?"

I felt a sudden jolt in my body. I didn't know how he had found out. I gulped and just as I was about to justify myself he stood up. He refused even to look my way as he spoke. "You lied to me? You know how I feel about lies Scarlet. I was out here making myself look like a fool for you. Doing everything for you and you just lied to me like it's nothing?"

I could tell that he was angry. I sighed as I walked closer to him and spoke. "Damien, I know it looks bad but please just hear me out. Just let me explain."

Just when I moved closer to him and tried to hold his hand he pushed me away instantly. I stumbled backward. He refused to look me in the eyes but I could see the hurt surfacing on his face.

"No, I don't want to hear anything from you. What on earth pushed you to lie to me? Why the hell couldn't you just be honest with me?"

I remained a few feet away from him still but in the moment I simply broke down and everything came storming out. All the feelings that I was keeping inside came out.

"Damien I didn't want to tell you the truth because they asked me to stay in Paris full time for at least the next two years. I'm carrying your child. I'm building a world with you and it scares me that if I start following my dreams, you will leave me behind. Your whole life is in the States. I can't ask you to let go of your life for me. I was just trying to make things work for the both of us because I have fought too long and too hard to be with you. I can't let a job or distance break us apart now!"

I watched as the look in his eyes shifted. He finally lifted his head and our eyes met for a moment. He ran his fingers through his hair as he spoke in a calmer tone.

"Scarlet if I was afraid of distance getting in between us I would have never sent those samples in. I would have never bought a place..."

He trailed off before he could go on as if he had spilled something he wasn't supposed to from his mouth. My eyes widened. I raised both my eyebrows in surprise as I spoke. "Wait, what do you mean bought a place? Damien what did you do?"

He stepped back and a small smile appeared on the corner of his lips as he shrugged his shoulders and spoke. "I told you Scarlet, I'm always thinking one step ahead and if you just put your trust in me you won't have to pull stunts like this and lie to me."

I sighed. Sometimes I truly didn't understand him. He took a small pause before he spoke again.

"Put some clothes on. You're coming with me."

My eyes were wide with surprise. I spoke up instantly. "Can you please tell me what the hell is going on Damien? I'm lost."

He shook his head as he grabbed his phone and he seemed to be furiously typing away. He didn't even look my way when he spoke. "Like I said, put your trust in me and you'll see. You won't have to worry about anything."

I knew that asking him further questions would be useless, so I hurried to the closet in the back of the hotel room. Damien had also thrown on a white button-up with his usual work pants. My eyes landed on a casual dress hanging in the wardrobe, and I threw it on with a long winter coat. As soon as I walked back to the center of the room, Damien offered me his hand as he spoke in a childish manner. "Hurry up princess, we have somewhere to be."

Our hands were clasped together as we ran through the halls of the hotel and I felt like my inner child was coming alive. I was giggling out loud and I could see the biggest smile spread across Damien's face. I knew we could only hold hands and be kids between the empty halls of the hotel and when we stepped out we would go back to hiding our relationship.

As we stepped out into the city with people bustling around and noise everywhere, Damien pulled me toward the sidewalk where a black Cadillac was parked. The windows were tinted. He opened up the door for me, and before I could even register what was happening, I saw someone unexpected.

Nana was sitting inside the car. A smile was painted upon her face and as soon as I saw her, a scream escaped my lips right away. I jumped forward and wrapped my arms around her. My body was flooding with excitement. She held on to me for a few moments before I turned to Damien with my eyes wide and filled with life as I spoke. "Was this the surprise? Oh my God! You actually flew Nana out here for me?"

He gestured for me to get into the car as he spoke. "This

isn't even half of the surprise, Scarlet. Get inside. We have a long way to go."

I had no idea what was going on but for the first time in a while I felt safe with just letting go and allowing Damien to take control. I turned to face Nana and spoke. "Nana, did you know about this the whole time?"

She pulled me closer to her and placed a kiss upon the side of my cheek as she gestured toward Damien. "Honey, the man has his way of making things work. I won't say more. You'll see."

I rolled my eyes at the both of them knowing that Damien had probably sworn her to secrecy.

The car ride felt like forever with suspense in the air. I had no idea where we were going but as far as I could see we had left the busy city behind and we were driving along the outskirts of Paris. Nana and Damien seemed to be enjoying the music in the car and watching the two of them bonding so well made my heart feel at peace.

It had taken us around three hours until the car finally came to a halt. My eyes were close to shutting. Just when I was about to drift off to sleep, Damien shook me by my shoulder and gestured toward the door as he spoke. "Come on babe, we're here."

It was around four in the morning. The sun was bound to rise in an hour to two. Nana and I stepped out of the car and at first all I could see were open fields all around me. I was confused at first. Flowers were blooming around the corners of the open land filled with grass. Damien took my hand slowly and began to turn me around.

My mouth fell open when I realized what exactly I was looking at.

"No way!" I tried to grasp what he had done.

Before me, a few feet away was what looked to be a

mansion surrounded with open fields. It was painted in white with black gates at the entrance. A guardhouse stood next to the gates and beyond them were gardens brimming with flowers.

I turned to face Damien and he spoke with a smile on his face.

"It's yours. I bought it for you. More like for us."

Tears were starting to form in the corners of my eyes. I couldn't believe it. He knew I was too overtaken by surprise so he spoke once again with my hands held in his.

"You don't have to worry about distance ever coming between us. I'm moving here with you Scarlet. You've sacrificed enough for me. It's my turn to make some changes now."

I looked around. My eyes landed on Nana and she offered me a soft nod. She knew exactly what was going on in my head. I turned to Damien and spoke with shock still washing over my face.

"What about your job? Bella? Everything?"

He smiled as he took a step closer to me and placed a kiss on my forehead. He seemed as calm as day as he spoke. "I own the company. I can run it from wherever I want. Bella already loves it here and what better place to raise a child of our own too if not around nature and a home full of love? Your Nana helped me find the place. She's going to live with us too and you won't have to worry about leaving her behind."

Tears were falling from my eyes as he pulled me close and my lips clashed with his.

I was still in shock when Nana's voice brought me back. "Come on you two lovebirds, let's show Scarlet the house from the inside!"

EPILOGUE
SCARLET

12 Months Later:

Getting a new job meant that Damien and I could live our lives out in the open without having to hide from the world. He was no longer my boss and things were finally falling into place.

Damien had proposed to me on our last night in Paris, but with a child on the way, and a new job, the wedding ceremony was put on hold until I had given birth to little Lucas. It was one of the most painful yet happiest days of my life.

It was like something out of a movie. My dream wedding.

And here I was, I could hear the chatter of the crowds in the distance. I was staring at myself in the wall-sized mirror before me. Anxiety was flooding through my body. A veil had been neatly placed upon my head. My blonde hair was curled perfectly. I couldn't believe I was staring back at myself in a custom-made designer wedding dress. The veil alone reached the end of the room. My dress perfectly fell over my body with embroidery upon the neckline. My collarbone was exposed and daisies were neatly held in my hands.

"You look like someone out of a dream, honey."

Nana stood behind me. I could see tears in her eyes. I turned around and just as I opened my arms to hug her she stepped away and spoke.

"You really want my makeup on your dress?"

I rolled my eyes and pulled her into a hug holding onto her as tightly as I could.

I heard the church bells ringing in the distance. Nana spoke with her voice breaking. "Go on! It's time for you to walk down that aisle."

I nodded. She offered me her hand and the doors leading to the aisle were opened up.

Live music was playing by an entire orchestra. Flowers were spread all around the open space. The wedding was taking place in New York. It was almost like a goodbye to the city that had made Damien the person he was today.

The skyline of New York was visible in the distance. Everyone was dressed in suits and gowns. Nana had taken my hand and I gripped on to her tightly. We walked down the cobblestone pathway leading to the front and I could see familiar faces in the crowd around me. As soon as we walked a little ahead my eyes landed on Damien. He stood at the end of the aisle dressed in a black suit perfectly tailored for his body. His hair was styled, his hands were neatly placed before him, and when his eyes landed on me, I could almost see the tears coming. He smiled. I approached him. The crowd roared in the background as he took my hand. We stood face to face and I could see the most beautiful future before me.

Bella entered right after bearing the rings. I knelt down and kissed her cheek. She did a little dance for the audience and laughter erupted in the background. Tory offered me a smile as she stood with the bridesmaids. She was holding little Lucas in her arms. The boy barely knew what was happening, but he seemed to be enjoying the music just like everyone else.

Then came the time to say our vows. Damien held both my hands as he spoke.

"Scarlet, I must say you took me by surprise. As I stand here proudly with your hands in mine, I must remind you I thank God every day I was in that bar the night I saw you for the first time. You have filled my life with color I never knew existed, and with every step you have taken by my side, you have made my heart grow fonder.

I promise to never leave your side, to always have take out with you in the living room after we put the kids to sleep, and to take you on fancy dates for the rest of your life. I promise to be your partner in crime, your lover, your best friend, and the man you can be always proud of calling yours."

The waterworks had started, and salty tears streamed down my cheeks. I barely heard when it was said we could kiss. Damien pulled me toward him, the crowd screamed, flowers were thrown into the air, fireworks went off that night across New York City, and every tabloid told the story of us.

The missing puzzle pieces had finally fallen into place, and we had managed to build a family, and a world of our own sheltered from the outside.

We had finally made it.

ALSO BY JEWEL STEIN

Do you like FREEBIE Romance books?

Sign up for my newsletter and get Grumpy Boss's Baby: An Enemies to Lovers Age Gap Romance for free @ https://BookHip.com/MZHGWSP

NEVER get knocked up by your older brother's bad boy best friend.

Even worse, he's also my rich grumpy boss.

It all started when he came to my rescue and pretended to be my boyfriend in front of my ex.

But the sparks that flew when he had his strong, protective arms
wrapped around me felt all too real.

Three days later, I'm starting my new dream job and he is
introduced as my boss.

The pull between us is undeniable, but completely off-limits.

But he doesn't care… He's made it clear that claiming me as his
own is his top priority.

The stakes are high - my brother would be furious if he knew.
And we could both lose our jobs.

Things are really messy, but they just got even messier…

I'm pregnant.

Sign Up Now!

Go to: https://BookHip.com/MZHGWSP

ABOUT THE AUTHOR

Jewel is a creative mind that loves to help people through the stories she creates. Her mantra in life just like in her books is that LOVE conquers all. Jewel is a wife and mom who in her spare time loves to travel, watch movies, try new recipes, and spend time with her family and friends.